ASK ME TO MARRY YOU

BRIDES OF EVERGREEN BOOK 2 CONTAINS THE STORIES A MALE-ORDER BRIDE AND A PROPOSAL SO MAGICAL

HEATHER BLANTON

RIVULET PUBLISHING

PART I

A MALE-ORDER BRIDE STORY

All rights reserved under International and Pan-American Copyright Conventions. By payment of the required fees, you have been granted the non-exclusive, non-transferable right to access and read the text of this e-book on-screen. No part of this text may be reproduced, transmitted, downloaded, decompiled, reverse engineered, or stored in or introduced into any information storage and retrieval system, in any form or by any means, whether electronic or mechanical, now known or hereinafter invented, without the express written permission of Rivulet Publishing or the author.

This novel is a work of fiction. Names, characters, places, incidents, and dialogues are either the product of the author's imagination or are used fictitiously. Any resemblance to actual events, locales, organizations, or persons, living or dead, is entirely coincidental and beyond the intent of the author.

Rivulet Publishing, LLC

Cover DESIGN by Ruthie, LLC

Scripture taken from the HOLY BIBLE

KING JAMES VERSION - Public Domain

A huge *thank you* to my editors: Kim Huther, Vicki Prather, Lisa Coffield; and my spectacular beta readers: Holly Magnuson, Vicki Goodwin, Becky Hrivnak, Loraine Ertelt, Rebecca Maney, Jessica Baker, Kristine Morgan, Heidi Varansky, Amy Fields, Noela Nancarrow, Liz Dent, , Lanna Webb, Laura Hilton, Pamela Morrisson, , Anne Rightler, Barbara Raymond, Janice Sisemore, Deanna stevens, Brittany McEuen, , Julia Wilson, Melissa Ahlersmeyer, Casey Heim, Jean Stewart, Kimberli buffaloe, Lisa Janey, Donita Corman, Rose Hale, Dotty Mathison, Carole Sanders, Linda Brooks, Connie White, Ruth Miller, Joyce Guard, Jessica Woodland, Adrienne Bowling, Heather Baker, Tiffany Gee, and Cathy Egland

And a huge shout-out to the awesome Diane Estrella! An author could not ask for a better, smarter, more dedicated assistant. Thank you! You are such a huge blessing!

Ask Me to Marry You

---

*Part I -- **"A Male-Order Bride"** With her father's passing, Audra Drysdale accepts she needs a man to save her ranch. A mail-order groom will keep her prideful men working and a neighboring rancher at bay. What could go wrong?*

*Part II -- **"A Proposal So Magical"** -- Evergreen's sheriff, Dent Hernandez, has fallen in love and now actually has to do something about it or risk losing the woman he loves.*

Heather Blanton

Please subscribe to my newsletter
By visiting www.authorheatherblanton.com
to receive updates on my new releases and other fun news.
You'll also receive a FREE e-book—
A Lady in Defiance, The Lost Chapters
just for subscribing!

**Wait on the LORD, and keep His way,
and He shall exalt thee to inherit the land:
when the wicked are cut off, thou shalt see *it*.**
Psalm 37:34

PROLOGUE

"Dear God, thank You for a wonderful ... day," Little Audra's eyes fluttered closed, but she blinked, trying to finish her prayers. She shifted on her knees and rested her head on her mattress. "Thank You for Pa taking me up to Powder River with him. Thank you for Cookie, the fastest horse alive." A yawn struck her. "Thank You for our ranch and the mountains and the wide-open spaces." On the verge of dozing, Audra smiled and her little heart swelled with contentment. "Oh, I love this ranch."

Her thoughts stopped for a moment as sleep softly pulled her into its warm embrace.

I love you, Audra, whispered the Lord. *What can I give you so you'll know I'm here?*

"Please don't let that mean Mr. Fairbanks ever get our place. I heard him fussing with Pa today."

This man shall not possess your land. Your very own husband will be your protector.

Audra smiled at the promise. It reminded her of the one He'd given to Abraham. She smiled even wider as big, familiar arms slipped around her and lifted her. "Here now, little gal, you can't sleep like that."

Pa. "I love you, Pa."

"I love you, too, punk." He kissed her forehead then slipped her beneath her covers. "Sleep tight. Don't let the bed bugs bite."

CHAPTER 1

Audra Drysdale threw down the empty bucket in disgust and just stood there. The heat from the burning barn, though, wouldn't allow her to stay. The flames hissed and snarled, driving her back. Wrestling a sob into silence, she turned her back on the inferno and trudged the hundred yards or so to the house.

She'd been warned. A woman alone couldn't run a ranch. When Bobby and Dale—her last two hands—got back from town and saw this, they'd quit her, too. For three months she'd fussed, fumed, fretted, and all but begged for her men to stay. To no avail. This would be the nail in the coffin.

She plopped down on the porch step, ready to wallow in misery and self-pity . . . only, that wasn't who she was. Her pa hadn't raised a quitter.

She'd prayed so hard these last several months, *God, You promised me. You said my own husband would be my protector. You said Fairbanks would never get this place. Please . . . save my ranch. You promised . . .*

Over and over she'd prayed for Him to do something. Pa had made her believe God didn't abandon His children, and that He had only good planned for them. Which was why Jess Fairbanks was not going to get her or this place. The dirty old man had laid his groping paws on her, trying to convince her to marry him. The memory made Audra's skin crawl.

God did not intend for her to marry him. She was certain of it.

Then what? What's the plan, God?

She lifted her gaze over the flames to the inky sky. No, she wouldn't marry Fairbanks, but a man *would* solve all her problems.

Winston Drysdale's law office always smelled of something cool, apple-mint tobacco maybe, and aged leather chairs. But her uncle's silence frustrated her. Audra drummed her fingers on the arm of the chair and waited for him to catch up.

He tapped his jaw, as if that might rattle understanding loose in his eighty-year-old brain. "Audra, I don't understand what you're asking me."

She'd too often been guilty of praying and then running out of patience, waiting for God to answer. But she really didn't think she was jumping ahead of Him this time. This plan made perfect sense—and the idea had to have come from God. "My barn burned down last night." She spoke a touch more slowly, hoping that would help. "I know Fairbanks is responsible. My last two hands are on the verge of quitting because they don't think I can protect them. I can keep my hands, even hire some back, if I produce a husband."

"*Produce* a husband?"

"And I'm sure that will make Fairbanks back off, too." Which was, perhaps, the bigger of the problems.

The grizzled old man merely blinked.

"Uncle," Audra sat up and laid her hand on his desk. "You bring wives out here for the ranch hands. I don't want to ship myself off to some man and leave my ranch. I want you to find me a man who will come here. I don't see any difference between a mail-order bride and a mail-order groom."

"Audra, dear, I do what I do because those boys can't read, and I don't want them thinking they have to settle for some gal from Kit's place. It's gratifying to be able to help them sort through the ads, read the responses. I find them nice girls to marry."

"So find me a nice husband. You're famous for your matchmaking."

"You want—no, *need*—you need a man who either has no home or is willing to leave his home. Those are not small hurdles. Nor do they recommend him as a prize catch."

"I don't have to marry a saint. It's a marriage on paper only. He'll have his own room. I just need a sort of proxy. Me in male form. Someone to give voice to the orders but, of course, I'll be running things."

Winston scratched his gray head, sending silver spikes in every direction. "You think having a man out at your place will get your boys to stay? And Fairbanks to let this go? You know he's wanted your ranch somethin' fierce for a good long time. And then when you blossomed into such a pretty thing . . ." He trailed off, sounding uncomfortable.

"He thought he would get the best of both worlds."

Winston's brow dipped. "Yes, and he's old enough to be your pa. Turns my stomach. Foolish old fart."

Audra batted her eyelashes at her uncle. "A husband would solve my problems."

"In the short term. Maybe." His pale blue eyes drilled into her. "Then what? You're gonna be saddled with a husband who is a perfect stranger. What if you can't stand him?"

"I thought about that. I want you to write up something that says the ranch is still mine. All mine."

"That agreement wouldn't be worth the paper it's written on. You know Wyoming property laws."

"No one would know that except an attorney. A year should be enough time to hire the hands back, straighten out Fairbanks, and get the ranch in top condition again. Then my husband can *abandon* me. I'll even give him a horse and maybe some seed money."

Winston rubbed his chin and sighed. "You're like a daughter to me, Audra. You know that. I can't let just anybody into your house, callin' himself your husband. I would have to find the right man, and that could take a considerable amount of time." Absently, he picked up a letter from his desk, glanced at it, but went back to it with keen interest, narrowing his eyes. "Maybe . . ." he whispered.

Curious, Audra leaned forward. "You've got someone?"

Exasperation deepened all the lines in her uncle's face. "If you aren't the biggest load of trouble your pa ever made." He sighed loudly. "I'll let you know something when I know something."

CHAPTER 2

Dillon Pine heard the clang of a jail cell door and jumped off his cot. His father had promised an attorney would be coming, but Dillon had *not* expected to sit in a Cheyenne jail for two solid days. Of course, this was no small charge, but still, *two* days? What good was money if it couldn't get a man out of jail quick-like? His father had probably dallied intentionally, an attempt to teach his wayward son a lesson.

He peered through the bars and down the hallway. A long, lanky old man in a black suit strode toward him. Dillon grinned with deep relief. "Winston, it's sure good to see you. I mean that, old friend." The two shook hands. "I was beginning to think I'd been forgotten."

The old man eyed the cell, looking amused by Dillon's predicament. "Pretty scroungy accommodations for a Pine." But the amused glow left his creviced face as he pulled a folded paper from his breast pocket. "But you may not like the terms for getting out any better."

"Anything would be bet—" Dillon stopped himself.

Winston was troubled and that didn't bode well. "Am I in that much of a mess?"

"Son, you're charged with conspiracy to commit murder. I might be able to get it reduced. In fact, I'm pretty confident that I can, but I could prove you were in *China* at the time of the murder and I'd say you're still looking at three to five years."

"What?" Dillon felt his heart stop. "That's crazy. I have an alibi. I was at O'Herlihy's and I have witnesses."

"The witnesses have recanted or gone missing. The O'Herlihy Brothers do not recall seeing you in their establishment."

Dillon's jaw dropped. "They're hanging me out to dry."

"Not exactly. They're just more interested in protecting one of their own."

"Three years." Devastated, Dillon stumbled over to his cot and collapsed onto it. "All I tried to do was buy some whiskey wholesale."

Winston let out a long, slow breath. "I have talked to the judge and offered him a deal. You plead guilty to a lesser charge and I'll get you probation. You have no prior arrests. You're not violent. Your family has a good name. A good name that we would all like to keep out of the papers. The judge and your father are agreeable."

Dillon looked up. "Sooo . . . I might not have to go to prison?"

"The terms of the probation are rather unusual. Not without some precedent, but you're not going to like them." The old man gave a here-goes-nothing shrug. "A young lady is in need of a husband. I recommended you."

Dillon stood up so fast his head nearly hit the lantern overhead. "What?" He lunged for the bars and grabbed hold. But panic gave way to rational thinking. Surely Winston was pulling his leg. He laughed with relief at his overreaction. "That's not funny. You had me going."

"It's no joke."

Time slowed to a crawl as Dillon tried to gauge the truth from the old man's somber expression. Realization brought no comfort. "You're crazy." He spun and paced in the cell. "That's not probation. That's ... that's ... obscene. It's slavery is what it is."

"Calm down." Winston patted the air. "Hear me out."

Pondering, Dillon scratched his eyebrow, licked his lips, swiped his hand over his mouth, and finally nodded. "Okay, but you're crazy. There's no way I'll agree to this."

"My brother passed away three months ago and left a successful cattle ranch to his daughter. A rival cattleman wants the place and thinks he can get it by running off her hands. The spineless, narrow-minded weasels don't want to work for a woman anyway, so all but two have left her. They're riding out tomorrow unless she comes home with a husband today."

Dillon was speechless for a moment, totally incapable of understanding the situation—the offer, or its ramifications. He decided to dismiss the offer with a wave. "I don't know anything about running a cattle ranch. Animal husbandry wasn't offered at Yale."

Winston didn't crack a smile. "Just what were you planning on doing with that fancy education?" He glanced around the cell again. "Seems a bit pointless now."

"I was buying a freight business. That's why I'm in Cheyenne." Dillon turned his back on Winston and walked over to the cell window. The Laramie Mountains looked so close, yet they'd never been so far away. He'd come home to open a business. Cheyenne was close enough to Denver that he could see his father, but not have to live with him, and maybe the two could work out their differences.

Getting arrested had sure put a chink in those plans. Three years in jail would destroy them. No matter the hard feelings, he couldn't do that to his father.

"What are the terms?" he asked without facing Winston.

"You will marry my niece and for one year be a model husband. She will tell you how to run the ranch and you will share those orders with the hands. At the end of the year, Audra believes she will have proven herself to the men as a competent rancher, despite her gender, and you may go on your way. She'll say you abandoned her and we'll quietly annul the marriage."

"A year is a long time."

"So is three to five. And the scandal would ruin your father..."

"Is she ugly? She must be ugly." He finally turned around. "That would be the icing on the cake."

"As a matter of fact she's quite beautiful, which brings us to the nitty gritty. She'll be quick to tell you this is a marriage in name only. Do you understand? Separate rooms." He lowered his voice. "She's like a daughter to me, Dillon."

"Well, this just keeps getting better and better." He came back to the bars. "Live like a monk and have a woman for a boss."

"Dillon, I believe that, in spite of your current circumstances and a few bad decisions, you are an honorable man. Otherwise, I wouldn't be here. This is an opportunity for you to stay out of jail, live quite comfortably for a time, and make new associations of a higher, less questionable quality. Possibly even mend fences with your father. And you will be helping a young woman who is in a tough spot. It is, nonetheless, probation. If you leave before the year is up, I'll have an arrest warrant issued, regardless of the scandal it would cause."

"Can I at least go to the saloon for a drink and a . . . *game* now and then?"

"You two can hammer that out, but I'm not sure she'd care, as long as you're discreet about it. Don't publicly shame her . . . in short, live quietly for a year. And do what she tells you." He raised a finger. "One other thing. I'm going to write up a prenuptial agreement that clarifies you hold no ownership in the ranch. When you leave, Audra will give you a horse and a thousand dollars."

"A thousand—?" That was enticing. He could put up with a lot of ugly for a nice stake like that. He wouldn't have to ask his father for the money the O'Herlihys stole, either. With a resigned sigh, he offered his hand through the bars.

CHAPTER 3

Audra had to admit she rather liked the sound of Dillon Pine's voice. Deep. Masculine. A touch velvety. Though, when he'd yelped, "What?" she'd had to slap her hand over her mouth to stifle a laugh.

She leaned against the wall in the outer hallway, sagging a little. Obviously, he wasn't thrilled with this idea. Well, neither was she. But she'd be danged if she'd lose her ranch just because men ran the world. Pa had thought the ranch hands would be all right with her taking the reins. She was, after all, more capable than any of them. She reached down and picked lint off her gauchos. Apparently no man wanted to be reminded that some women didn't *need* a man.

She straightened up, refusing to lose herself in bitterness. She'd show them. She'd show them all.

"Audra?" Winston poked his head around the corner. "Would you like to meet Dillon?"

Her heart took off at a gallop. "Not really." She smiled weakly at the bad joke. After all, this was her mess. On rubbery legs, she slogged down the hallway, Winston leading the way. He stopped at a cell. Two clean, masculine hands hung outside the bars. Audra took a breath and stepped where she could see the man they belonged to.

Dillon Pine was not ugly. He had eyes so blue they seemed to glow, and wavy black hair that touched his collar. He was tall, too, and lean, but not skinny. She could argue he was very manly. Manly enough to pass for a ranch owner.

They stared at each other awkwardly for a moment then Dillon offered his hand. "Miss Drysdale."

"Mr. Pine."

The handshake lingered and Audra wasn't sure whose fault it was. Blushing as they broke apart, she laced her hands behind her back. "This is very awkward. I don't really know what to say."

"I thought you came to ask me to marry you."

A maddening little grin played around the man's lips and Audra had the burning desire to slap it right off his face. "Is this a joke to you?"

"No, ma'am. It may be a lot of things—foolish, stupid, hare-brained—but it's definitely not a joke."

Audra didn't know how to take Mr. Pine. She glanced over at Winston, pleading silently with him to make this awkward situation bearable.

He stepped a little closer, as if getting the message. "I think all I need to hear from the both of you is yea or nay. If it's yea, I'll get Dillon released and we'll find us a justice of the peace back home in Evergreen."

Mr. Pine's eyes widened. "A justice of the peace?" He looked at Audra. "You have something against preachers?"

"Of course not. I merely prefer to save that for a real wedding. This is a formality."

He seemed to ponder that, then his gaze traveled over her, top to bottom and back again. "Yeah. All right. I guess I can see your point." He laced his hands together. "I have a couple of questions first."

She nodded slightly, giving him the go-ahead.

"Can you cook?"

Audra assumed he wanted to know how well he would be eating for the next year. "I'm a passable cook. Some would say better than fair."

"And you know I don't know anything about running a ranch."

"Yes. Can you at least ride? A horse?"

His lips twitched. "I can stay in the saddle. Can I drink?"

"I don't know. Can you?"

"I mean," he lowered his voice, "if I want to visit the saloon, have a drink, play a little poker, that's agreeable?"

"Are you a drunk or a whoremonger?"

He laughed. "No. Drunks and whoremongers don't make it through Yale."

"Yale?" She looked at Winston.

"Yeah, he has a fancy education. Give him a little whiskey and he'll talk your ear off—in Latin."

"What did you study?"

"Business and Political Science."

Audra was both impressed and shocked. And just maybe she could put that fancy education to use, at least for a little while. "How did you wind up in so much trouble?"

His face darkened a bit and she felt she'd overstepped, but then again, if she was going to *marry* the man, she had a right to ask.

He sighed. "Let's just say my fancy education doesn't change the laws regarding stolen property, corruption, and vice."

She studied him for a moment, debating hard. But what choice did she have? "Are you prone to fits of anger?"

He shrugged. "No more than any other man."

Audra didn't find that reassuring. She did, however, trust Winston. "Fine."

Dillon tilted his head. "I'm sorry. I'm not sure I understand. Isn't there something you want to *ask* me?"

"Ask you?" Audra's cheeks heated, but not from embarrassment. What a pompous— "Would you like to stay out of jail? Do you prefer probation to incarceration? That what you mean?"

He shook his head. "No. That's not it." He strolled over to the cot and sat down. "If I'm going to have a woman lording over me for a year, well, I need—"

"Your ego soothed?" Audra fumed. Men. Was there a creature more shallow in the world? "Your feathers unruffled? Well, I didn't put you in here, Mr. Pine, but I can get you out."

"That's right. You can." He stood again and strode over to the bars. He leaned toward her, as close as the iron would allow. "With one little question."

They stared at one another. Unblinking. Audra teetered between lamenting this mess and admiring Dillon's swagger. And enticing blue eyes.

She blinked. *Anything for my ranch.* "Fine. Will you marry me, Mr. Pine?"

A slow, easy grin raised the corner of his mouth. "You can call me sweetheart."

CHAPTER 4

*I*n the tiny courtroom in Evergreen's town hall, Winston snagged Sheriff "Dent" Hernandez and a cowhand paying a fine, to act as witnesses. Audra's heart beat out of her chest as the Justice of the Peace said the words to a simple ceremony.

She repeated *this isn't real, it's just for show* over and over in her head, but when the justice of the peace pronounced them man and wife, she felt a terrible explosion of panic. *Oh, Lord, what have I done?*

"You may kiss the bride."

She and Dillon leaned toward each other, then backed away, shock and confusion on their faces. Awkwardly, he shoved out his hand. Dent snorted at the absurd gesture. Audra didn't know what to do and stared at Dillon, horror and humiliation washing over her. Winston cleared his throat and bobbed his chin slightly. Though this was a lie, a charade, people had to believe she was married.

She closed her eyes and lifted her face to Dillon. The time felt like an eternity until his lips pressed against hers. Warm and gentle. Then his hand came to rest lightly on her cheek.

Something inside her sparked to life. Her breathing hitched and her legs suddenly felt all wobbly. He deepened the kiss—

"Congratulations, you two," Winston said, stepping forward quickly.

Heart pounding like a stampeding herd, Audra pulled away from Dillon, but didn't miss the mischief in his eyes. Or was that desire?

The wedding dampened their spirits, or at least ended the cocky banter. Audra settled on the buggy seat beside Dillon, quiet as a church mouse. He hadn't uttered a word to her since the ceremony, and she was too unnerved to talk.

"Where to?" he asked, lifting the reins.

"West out of town." She turned and smiled down at Winston. "Thank you for everything."

"I'll be checking on you. I just hope—" Winston's gaze shot passed her. He pointed with his chin and she followed his stare. "Speak of the devil." Dent was talking to Jess Fairbanks in front of the bank and motioned toward them a few times.

"Looks like news of your nuptials is going to get around pretty darn fast."

She glared at the old cattle baron, his wavy silver hair shining like a beacon, the conchos on his gun belt glinting in the sun. In his sixties, he was still as salty as a young man in his thirties, or so he liked to think. He was arguably handsome, but he was also sinister and brooding. And unaccustomed to hearing the word *no*. He'd made the point abundantly clear to Audra, who was a little unsettled by his aggressiveness. Still, he was a harmless, if not frisky, old goat.

"He's a cocky-looking old rooster," Dillon said, studying the man. "Wears that gun belt like a real desperado."

"'Bout as friendly as one, too." Audra had every intention of avoiding introductions, but Jess slapped Dent on the back, stepped down into the street, and headed straight for her.

"So, is this him? I hear Winston there went and found you a mail-order bride?"

Audra gasped and a mean smile cut across Jess's face. Beside her, Dillon's fingers tightened on the reins.

"How Audra went about getting a husband is of no concern to you, Jess." Winston walked around the back of the buggy to stand in front of him. "You could wish them good luck."

Jess wouldn't take his cold, hazel eyes off Audra. "Why did you go and do a fool thing like this?"

"I'm in love. Isn't that why folks get married?"

After a moment, he finally tore his gaze away from her to survey Dillon. "What's your name?"

Dillon flexed his fingers. "You know, Fairbanks, if I were a lesser man and if this wasn't my wedding day, I would take strong offense to the way you're talking," he leaned forward a little, "to my wife."

Jess's eyebrow twitched a hair. His face tightened up like he had lockjaw. In no hurry, he slid his baleful stare back to Audra. "You've just gone and made things a whole lot harder than they had to be."

With a slap to the buggy, he turned and headed back toward the bank. Winston shook his head in resignation. He gave the happy couple a sad little smile and wandered off in the opposite direction.

*D*illon snapped the reins and pointed the horse out of town. "Winston could have told me I'm stepping into a hornets' nest." He'd been pretty upfront about everything else, including warning him what a breath-taker Audra was.

"But you're not, at least not now, anyway. I'm married. Now that there's a man around, he won't try anything else."

"Else? What's he done up to now?"

"I'm pretty sure he burned my barn. And he convinced my hands I can't run the ranch or protect them."

"Now, *that* I don't understand. I can understand not wanting to work for a woman, but how are you supposed to protect *them*?"

"Men ride for the brand, if you're a good boss and earn their loyalty. One gets hurt, all the boys come a-runnin'. Jess convinced them I wouldn't be able to stand up for them."

"That sounds like he threatened them."

"No . . ." Audra faded off.

Dillon snuck a sideways glance and saw the doubt on her face. What if this Fairbanks had done more than sow doubts about her as a boss? What if he had threatened her hands, either directly or through subtle hints? Did Winston know, or at least suspect, Audra was in over her head with the neighbor? "How did your father die?"

"His horse threw him."

"Did you see it?"

"As a matter of fact, I did." Her eyebrows dove, expressing her disapproval of the question. "I think you're letting your imagination run away with you if you think Jess is that dangerous. Stubborn, greedy, heavy-handed—but he's no murderer."

"People can be unpredictable, Audra, more than you'd think. Especially when it comes to getting money and power.

Your uncle told me how big your ranch is. It's gotta be worth a lot of money."

"I promise Jess is not a problem anymore. And with you around, I can pull the Diamond D back together. I can rehire the hands who left, find a good foreman, and I'll earn their respect."

"If you couldn't earn their respect when your father was alive, what's different now?"

"Brains. Pa wouldn't let me show them I had any brains about ranching. It's going to be different with you. I'll have to help you. As far as the men are concerned, we're running the ranch together. Just do what I tell you and we'll be fine."

Do what I tell you. Those words grated on his nerves like sandpaper. The very words that had caused him so much trouble before and during college. Now they were coming from a woman who was pretending to be his wife, so she could be his boss. He had swallowed some big pills in his life, but this was the biggest, most bitter one yet. He slapped the reins and moved the horse up to a trot as they left Evergreen behind. "One year," he muttered under his breath. "One year."

CHAPTER 5

Dillon tossed his one bag on the log bed and sighed.

"Can you meet me at the barn in a few minutes?"

He heard the hesitancy in her voice. It mirrored how he felt right now—doubtful, unsure, on guard. *Just keep telling yourself this is better than prison.*

He rounded on her and shrugged, shoving his hands into his pockets. "What's wrong with now?"

She wrung her hands. "I thought you might want a minute—"

"To stare at the walls and wonder what I've gotten myself into? Reflect on what a bad idea this is?"

"You think it is?"

The sincere hope in her eyes caught him off guard. Winston sure was right about her. Audra was a stunning beauty. Green eyes, wide and cool, watched everything. She wore her long golden hair pulled back in a no-nonsense braid. Her lifted chin and straight, square shoulders said she was ready for a fight. Feisty, yes, but unsure of things at the moment. He'd second-guess this decision too, if he was her.

He sucked in a breath. "It's gotta be better than prison, right?"

She deflated a little and he wished he had said something more encouraging.

"When we get outside, I think you should tell Bobby and Dale to get started on the barn. Then I'll show you the ranch."

---

*T*wo cowboys waited at the corral. One lanky fella draped himself over the fence; the other, shorter and pudgier, sat on a bale of hay, chewing on a piece of straw. Behind them, the blackened skeleton of the barn lay in a heap. Dillon spotted a flatbed wagon off to the side loaded with a pile of fresh lumber.

"Bobby, Dale, I'd like you to meet my husband, Dillon Pine."

Husband? Dillon nearly gaped but caught himself. He wasn't used to the word, or the role. To their credit, the two men recovered from their own shock quickly and extended their hands.

"Howdy," Bobby said.

The straw had fallen out of Dale's mouth, but clung to his chin. "Good to know you," he said, reinserting it.

They shook hands and Dillon smiled, trying to make the expression real. "Hello. Nice to meet you both. Miss Audra speaks very highly of you." The ranch hands puffed up like roosters. Noting the response, Dillon poured on a little more honey. "You've stood by her. I appreciate that."

"Yes, sir," Bobby pushed his hat back. "Miss Audra is a fine lady, but she knows we're glad to have a man around again."

"For a couple of reasons," Dale muttered.

"Mr. Pine has a lot to learn about ranching, boys," Audra

interjected, "but we'll teach him. Right now, I—we—" She motioned to Dillon. "That is, after discussing the plans for today..." She twirled her hand.

He got the cue. "You two get started on the barn. My wife is going to give me the penny tour."

"Yes, sir," the two echoed and jerked on their work gloves double time. Dillon didn't miss the indignant look Audra gave the men, as if they never moved that fast for her.

"Dale, why don't you saddle up Daisy for Mr. Pine here? Until we know how well he rides, she's the best choice."

Daisy? All three of the men exchanged puzzled glances, but Dillon got the point. Audra had something to prove and it would have to be at his expense. He didn't have to go along easily, though. "I appreciate your concern, dear. Daisy will be fine for the time being. I can, however, saddle my own horse, Dale. You two go on and tackle the barn."

The men nodded and left.

Dillon folded his arms over his chest and gave Audra a hard look. "This how it's gonna be? Beat me down to lift yourself up."

She shifted on her feet, looking away. "I figure it has to be this way. You saw. I'm walking a fine line between respect and failure here."

"You're not the only one."

"But it doesn't matter if they see you as weak or incompetent. Just by virtue of your gender, you're instantly seen as more competent than I am." She glared at the men lifting wood from the wagon. "I have to make a dent in that idea."

And Dillon was just supposed to put up with the *dented* pride? *Fine.* He could do it. For a year. The time would fly by...

"Fortunately, we keep all the feed and the tack here instead of the barn." Audra plucked reins, bridles, and bits from the storage shed's wall.

Dillon ran his hand over a fine Fred Mueller saddle hanging from a rack, a beautiful thing of rich black and red leather with a padded suede seat and intricate tool work.

Audra came to stand beside him and gently caressed the pommel. "That was my pa's." She tugged on the stirrup of the one hanging above it, a worn, simple, no-frills saddle. "Use this one."

Dillon lamented not getting to use that high-end saddle and the Navajo blanket it sat on, but he understood and would go along.

It wasn't like he had much of a choice.

CHAPTER 6

*D*illon lowered himself into the tub of hot water and sighed with sublime contentment. Not a bone in his body didn't ache. He'd never spent so many hours in the saddle, not even back at school practicing with the polo team.

Audra, on the other hand, belonged on a horse. Flowing and natural, she rode like the animal was an extension of her body. At one point her braid had come loose during a canter over a ridge, and her blonde hair had poured out behind her like a golden waterfall. Truly, there had been moments when he couldn't take his eyes off her.

She was a masterpiece, as gorgeous as any work of art in a museum.

Only she was a real, living, breathing woman.

"Oh, no you don't," he chastised himself aloud. "Uh-uh. No getting caught in that." He grabbed the soap and lathered up. "A year. You get to play cowboy and then you're done. Remember, it's house arrest. No touching the jailer."

"Dillon?" Audra knocked on his door. "Dinner will be ready in thirty minutes. Hope you're hungry."

Food. Yes, food. He would focus on that hunger and . . . not the other.

Since Dillon had to admit Audra was beautiful enough to shame Venus di Milo, and could ride, rope, and herd cattle like a man, he halfway suspected she could cook like a chef. He took a bite of her Beef Wellington and almost groaned with pleasure. *Suspicion confirmed.* He hadn't exactly been eating in the finest establishments in Cheyenne, as he'd been busy chasing down some wholesale products. Not to mention two days in jail had certainly whet his appetite for good food, but the Wellington was a sensual explosion of flavor in his mouth.

Audra sat down opposite him, her face angelic, her expression hopeful in the lantern's amber light.

He swallowed and tried not to think about appetites of any kind. "It's very good. You're a fine cook."

"Thank you, but I thought you might say grace."

"Oh, I don't—"

"That's fine." She smiled, a little sadly, he thought. "I'll say it."

She blessed the meal then scooped her own serving. She poked at it for a moment, instead of tasting it. "I know this is just a business arrangement—us, I mean—but I thought a special meal was in order."

"I'm glad you thought so." He closed his eyes and savored another bite. "Truly glad."

"Good." They ate quietly for a few minutes, but he could tell by her tapping fingers on the water glass she was searching for a way to start conversation. "So, Uncle Winston told me a little about you, but I was wondering, why did you go back East?"

The Wellington lost a little of its flavor and he washed it down with a splash of coffee. "Did he tell you who my father is?"

She shrugged a shoulder. "Another lawyer down in Denver is all he said. And that they've been friends a long time."

Now Dillon poked at his food. "I can be a little headstrong, I suppose. My father and I had a falling-out. He wanted me to be an attorney, too. I want to be a businessman. Our last *discussion* ended badly. I left for Yale and didn't come back until three months ago."

"So you never visited your parents the whole time you were in school?"

"My mother came twice. She was unhappy with how I was conducting myself. But she wrote me, regardless." He could tell Audra wanted to ask more questions and, in fairness, his vague language did leave the door open for them. "I suppose since we're married, you should know a thing or two about me. I put myself through school by gambling, doing a little boxing. Mother was disappointed. I didn't tell her Father had opted not to pay for my education, and I had no desire to return to Colorado without one."

He took a bite of the beef, chuckling at how angry and determined he'd been those first few years of school. "I had no intention of ever returning at all."

"What changed?"

"The O'Herlihy Brothers knew people in Cheyenne who wanted items stored and shipped. I wanted to start my own freight business. They agreed to send me some customers. I agreed to cut rates if they paid in whiskey." He stared through his plate. "Not the best idea I've ever had."

"Pa told me once you can tell a lot about a man by who he's willing to do business with."

Dillon thought the observation was harsh, but mostly

true. He hoped in his case it was wrong. "I'd like to think that one bad choice is not a reflection of how smart I really am. I suppose I could be wrong, though." An awkward silence fell and Dillon went back to his meal.

"I'm sorry," she said. "I didn't mean for that to be a cut."

"No, it's fine. Who knows. Maybe I would have kept going down a road filled with bad choices if I hadn't been caught up in the gang's mess."

"Yes, I suppose marrying a strange woman doesn't qualify as a bad decision." She laughed and he echoed it, this time with real humor.

"It does sound bad when you say it out right."

Their laughter died and they looked at one another. What kind of decision would this turn out to be? He suspected they were both pondering that very question.

"I play poker," she said unexpectedly.

His eyes bugged. "Do you?"

"Rancher's daughter. Not a lot to do on long, cold winter nights. Pa was good, but I was better."

"How do you know he didn't let you win?"

Grinning, she rose and sauntered over to the fireplace. She pulled down a deck of cards and a box and set them on the table. The box was full of poker chips. "Let's find out."

The game lasted for a while. Dillon noticed that Audra was not eager to talk about herself, but she talked about the ranch with great enthusiasm. And she was impressively well-versed in the running of it. She rattled off numbers, historical figures, and projections like a Wall Street businessman. She talked at length about the plans for the Diamond D, her goals for building a larger herd, and her dream of running a fine horse ranch here as well.

All while cleaning Dillon out of a hundred dollars. He'd never enjoyed losing money more. What a conundrum she was. A girl who could play poker with the best of them, yet said grace at dinner. He could make a pastime out of trying to figure her out. He doubted, however, a year would be long enough.

CHAPTER 7

*A*udra supposed it might take several nights to get used to having Dillon in the house. Or at least that was her rationalization for why she couldn't sleep. She had enjoyed playing poker with him, the game a temporary reprieve from her grief. This was the first time she'd had company since her father passed. She longed to hear his gruff voice just once more, telling her to saddle up and get a move on.

But Dillon, he seemed to feed a different kind of longing, one that puzzled her. How many times during the game had her gaze wandered to his lips, his freshly shaved jaw? She'd noticed he ran his hand through his dark, wavy hair every time he debated a bluff. He caressed a card gently when he had a terrible hand. She was fascinated with his hands . . . clean, lean, strong . . .

Huffing a frustrated sigh, she threw the covers back and quietly wandered out to the front porch in her nightgown. The inky black sky covered in glittering diamonds, the mysterious Milky Way, and shooting stars disappearing behind the mountains always filled her with such a sense of wonder. Yes, she felt small and insignificant, yet loved by a God Who had created an amazing vista. If she had her ranch and these stars, she'd always count herself blessed.

"It is a sight."

She squeaked like a terrified mouse when Dillon moved in the rocking chair to her right. She folded her arms, even though the gown was quite modest.

"Sorry." He rose and walked over to her, carrying a lit cigar. "I couldn't sleep."

"No, it's fine. I'm not used to having anyone here, is all. I hope my cooking or the bed isn't the problem."

"Nope. It's all very," he took a puff, exhaled it slowly, "comfortable." He didn't necessarily sound pleased.

"Should I say I'm sorry?"

He waved the glowing cigar. "I just meant, I'm . . ." he grunted. "Never mind. It'll take a little getting used to, but it's just—"

"Just for a year?"

Whereas the length of time had seemed so insignificant before, now Audra glimpsed the dangers ahead.

"Tell me how you see this playing out," he said, hooking his thumb in his belt loop, the cigar glowing orange. "How do I run this ranch?"

She rubbed her arms, the cool summer night raising gooseflesh. "I guess I imagined I would ride everywhere with you but quietly make the decisions. You deliver them."

"You're the ventriloquist and I'm the dummy?"

"I—I . . ." That sounded horrible. "No, that's not right."

"Maybe it is a fair trade for prison. Small price to pay, my pride, I mean."

Audra had no idea what to say to that. It *did* seem like a small price to her. After all, this really wasn't going to be that painful, not compared to actual *prison*. She had half-a-mind to be annoyed with him going on about his pride.

Men. "I'm going back to bed. Goodnight."

He mumbled goodnight around the cigar in his mouth.

A week later, Dillon could argue he and Audra had started settling into a routine of sorts. At least their time together went a bit more smoothly. At breakfast they discussed basic ranch management, stock yields, expenses, and so on. They touched on the daily chores required on a ranch, which included finishing the barn and riding sections of fence. They fed stock together so he could get a feel for feed requirements, and she'd given him a tour of the land near the ranch house.

The more he learned, the more Dillon caught himself thinking that ranching was more a business and less a seat-of-your-pants venture. A quick glance at Audra's books spoke volumes about ways to improve stock yields and cut expenses. Ideas thundered through his head like a herd of stampeding cattle. But he couldn't take anything away from her. Audra knew how to run a ranch. Her business sense was impressive, especially considering she'd never attended college.

Today, the *happy couple* saddled up and headed off for a special ride, or so the little missus had called it.

"We're going to ride a section it's important you see." Audra kicked Cookie into a canter, and Dillon did an admirable job keeping up with her without being showy. While he resented being relegated to second fiddle, he despised the constant urge to prove his manliness and decided to keep his ego—and his own equestrian skills—in check. Even if it was like chewing on nails.

They'd ridden for half an hour or so when she finally said, "It's important a rancher knows where his boundaries are."

"How much land do you have exactly?"

"Right now, I'm holding on to twelve hundred acres."

Dillon whistled. "That's a nice size plot."

"I wish it were bigger. To put it in perspective, Jess Fairbanks owns three times that. And that's one of the things I wanted to show you."

Another hour of riding passed and Audra showed no signs of slowing. The land around them was wide open, hilly, and dotted with dense, deep-green pine forests. Towering mountains, hazy and blue, surrounded the valley. The clean cedar-scented air struck a homey chord in Dillon. Maybe he would go visit Denver sooner rather than later.

His gaze crept over to Audra, her hips rocking fluidly in the saddle, her ornery jaw softened by a smile. He smiled, too, knowing he was enjoying this almost as much as she seemed to be.

"This makes our arrangement a little easier to swallow."

"You like riding?" She sounded surprised.

He looked around. "I like riding out here. I feel like I could keep going till I hit the Yellowstone."

"There's only one problem with that. Follow me." She turned her horse due west.

After several minutes of watching her and wondering about his *bride*, Dillon risked learning a little about her. He considered it a risk because he wasn't sure if he should venture too near the fire. "Have you ever been outside of Wyoming?"

"Sure. I've been to Colorado and Utah."

"You ever been to any big cities, like New York or San Francisco?"

"Nope."

"And you don't think you're missing anything, either, do you." It wasn't a question. He'd never seen a person, male or female, more born to ranch, to ride the high country and the plains. Audra had found her destiny and he envied her. "You don't think one day you'll feel like you should have done more with your life?"

She cut him a sideways glance and smirked. "Wait till you see this and you'll know the answer."

She led him up a steep hill. Navigating around massive boulders, cedars, and pines, they emerged on top of a high and long butte. The view took his breath away. In the far distance, snow-tipped mountains reached unchallenged for the sky. Much closer, rolling green hills and valleys spread from horizon to horizon. A ribbon of aquamarine snaked its way through the center of the landscape.

Home. The space. The big sky. How he had missed the mountains and the plains. He could live if he never saw the East again. It made him wonder why he'd ever left in the first place.

"That river down there is the border between my ranch and Fairbanks's. Neither of us controls it; we share the water. The grass, though, is better on my side because of the runoff."

"And he's crossed over, has he?"

"Repeatedly. But now that you're here . . ."

"Now that I'm here, he'll back off?"

"That was my plan."

Dillon heard the uncertainty, and thought immediately of the veiled warning Fairbanks had issued in town. "You could be right."

But he suspected the opposite. Jess Fairbanks struck him as a man who didn't stand down till the fight was finished. Near as Dillon could tell, it hadn't gotten started good . . . not yet.

CHAPTER 8

For all his faults, Dillon did not shirk work, a source of pride to him. A competent carpenter, he jumped in and helped Bobby and Dale on the barn, listening carefully to their conversations. He learned a fair amount about cattle as they assessed the condition of the herd and expressed their longing to get back into the saddle.

A few times they had tentatively asked him questions about his background, but he'd turned them down some side roads, or climbed a little higher on the ladder and pretended not to hear.

Busy nailing down cedar shingles, Dillon caught sight of Audra leading a horse out to the corral and paused to watch her lunge the filly. He didn't even notice the hot July sun beating down on him. She and the horse were things of beauty, their work together magical.

A few feet down from him Bobby stopped, too, and whistled. "Look at her, would ya? My, she's a pretty little thing, ain't she? I bet a man could fall asleep on top of her."

"Hey," Dillon tossed a nail at Bobby to get his attention.

"If you're talking about my wife, I reckon there's going to be a fight."

The man's eyes bugged and his cheeks flushed bright red. "Holy cow, Mr. Pine, I would never. I was talkin' about that little filly and her smooth gait."

Dillon chuckled and went back to work, but, oddly, he felt a sense of relief that the young ranch hand didn't have eyes for the boss's wife.

"Hey, boss," Dale hollered from below. "Rider comin'." He pointed off behind Dillon.

Dillon turned carefully on the ladder and scanned the open hills. He spotted the man coming in at an easy lope, but couldn't identify him. He hung his hammer in his belt and climbed down. Dipping his bandanna in the rain barrel, he wiped off some sweat as he walked around to the front of the barn.

The man entered the gate and slowed to a trot. Dillon's eyes narrowed when he saw the visitor carrying flowers. Somehow, he knew they weren't for Audra.

She stopped her horse and waited, but the cowboy ignored her and rode straight for Dillon. "You Mr. Pine?" Steely gray eyes and a smirk delivered a clear message.

"I am."

"Compliments of Mr. Fairbanks." The cowboy tossed the bouquet, long white ribbons trailing. Dillon caught it with one hand. "He heard you didn't have a bouquet at your wedding. Said every mail-order bride ought to have flowers."

Off in the distance Dillon heard Bobby and Dale snort, then hide it with coughing. Heat rushed to his face and he lost the fight to stop a sneer. "Tell Fairbanks he's poking the bear."

"You mean bride, don't ya?"

Audra ran up, snatched the flowers away from Dillon,

and threw them at the rider, who swatted down the missile. Petals rained to the ground.

"Get out of here and don't come back." Her gloved hands curled into little tight fists. "You're not welcome here. And remind Jess he isn't either."

The man's grin widened. "She does your fightin' for ya too." Chuckling, he tugged on the reins and rode back the way he'd come.

Dillon ground his teeth as he glared at the flowers on the ground. He was the biggest joke in the county. Livid, he turned his glare on Audra. "Just what do you think you were doing? Oh, wait," he tapped his temple then snapped his fingers. "Running everything. Well it may surprise you to learn I can fight my own battles, *Mrs. Pine.* Your meddling is not helpful."

Startled, she stepped back, but embarrassment overtook her surprise. She brushed a sweaty strand of golden hair out of her eyes and nodded. "I'm sorry. I guess I overstepped."

"By about a mile." He lowered his voice, "You want this marriage to look real, quit stepping on my toes and let me lead."

CHAPTER 9

That night was quiet, even more than when Audra had actually been alone in the house. She'd suffered through a tense dinner with Dillon, their conversation limited to work subjects, his responses short and clipped. She'd apologized again, but he'd merely stared at her and whispered, "One year."

At a loss on how to restore civility between them, she'd taken a bath in the back room, then settled by the fireplace with her Bible. Her attention, however, kept wandering to Dillon's door.

She couldn't find the right balance for this marriage. She had to lead because she was the one in need of respect, not him. Yet, it almost hurt watching him get humiliated by Jess's man.

A wedding bouquet, of all things.

Oh, Lord, please forgive me, but the next time I see Jess Fairbanks I'm going to shove a daisy in his mouth.

She pinched her brow and sighed. The Psalms couldn't comfort her if she was going to harbor that kind of attitude. She'd hoped reading her Bible in front of Dillon might get him to ask some questions about her faith, but lately she'd been a poor witness. Properly humbled, she decided to try apologizing again.

She rapped softly on Dillon's door. No answer. She tried again, a little louder. Slowly, she pushed open his door. "Dillon, I just wanted to say . . ." Light spilled into his room.

It was empty.

This whole time she'd thought he was in here, but he must have slipped out while she was bathing.

She rested her shoulder against the frame, unable to deny the sadness that gripped her.

This was going to be one long year.

---

*A*udra poured Dillon's coffee and smiled at him, hoping to erase some of the tension between them. "I knocked on your door last night."

Dillon's eyebrow lifted and his lips twitched.

"To apologize again." His almost-pleased look made her hands shake. Flustered, she plopped down in front of her own plate. "You weren't there."

"I was out in the shed cleaning tack."

Relief warmed her, but she tried to blame it on the coffee. He hadn't gone to Kit's Place. "I have to go into town today, if you'd like to ride along."

He didn't smile back, but he nodded. "I could use some different scenery."

---

*S*he tried a little small talk on the way but Dillon was still resistant, as if he was keeping a tight grip not just on the reins, but his mood as well. Finally, she decided to make a serious attempt at humbling herself. "I'm sorry you've become the butt of some jokes. I'll try to let you . . ."

"Be a man?"

So his ego was the crux of the matter, and she'd inadvertently done everything she could to crush it. "I didn't realize . . ." Embarrassed all over again at her insensitivity, she shook her head. "I am pretty dense, I guess. I should have figured, in a small town . . . Uncle Winston doing what he does . . . you not being from around here, people would put two and two together."

"And come up with three. But we can't exactly tell them you plucked me out of jail, either."

She tickled the palm of her hand with her braid. "I suppose not."

A long minute passed before he finally spoke again. "Maybe I'm being too sensitive. Jokes eventually die down. Egos heal."

Aware he was making a peace offering, she let out a breath. "You're probably already forgotten."

---

*F*ive minutes into town, that proved not to be the case.

Snorts and giggles followed Dillon and Audra down the street. Two cowboys standing in front of the saloon hummed "Here Comes the Bride" as they rolled by. Audra flinched. Dillon's face hardened and turned nearly purple. What could she say? There was no doubt who was being taunted.

"You know, prison is looking better and better. At least there's no question I'm a man there."

Anger sparked in Audra. "We can always change our minds about this, Dillon. Prison isn't going anywhere."

With swift, frustrated movements, he pulled the team over to the boardwalk and handed Audra the reins. "Don't wait around." He saluted good-bye and jumped down. "I'll find my own way home."

"Wait, where are you going?"

He stopped with his back to her. "To drink, smoke, play cards, and do anything else that a man does to feel like a man." With that he stomped off, the echo of his boots thudding against her ears . . . and her heart.

CHAPTER 10

Dillon trudged down the stairs of Kit Calloway's saloon, halfheartedly keeping time with the piano player banging out "Buffalo Gals." He'd had every intention of letting the gal in room 201 work out the kinks in his twisted ego. Not a man given to visiting soiled doves, he'd felt pushed into smoothing out his pride. Yet, lying down on the brass bed, all he'd done was think about the pretty little, God-fearing *wife* he'd left back home.

For some reason, the soiled dove—Missy, was it?—she'd been content to listen. And Dillon had talked. A lot. A half-a-bottle of whiskey and he'd rattled on about his fake marriage, his probation, and, worse, Audra. He'd shamed her by coming here. He'd shamed her by closing Missy's door, regardless of what *didn't* happen. People would talk.

Sure another shot would wash down the guilt—*puzzling* guilt, seeing as how he was not actually married to Audra—he bellied up to the bar and ordered a whiskey. It burned and softened the inexplicable nagging of his conscience, but didn't silence it.

He had every right to be here. He didn't owe Audra

ASK ME TO MARRY YOU

anything and he certainly hadn't betrayed any vows. They were both doing each other a favor. Simple as that.

He stared at his reflection in the mirror behind the bar and recalled that wedding-day kiss. He'd never had a kiss haunt him before, but it came back often, especially when they studied the accounting books together or worked shoulder to shoulder rolling out barbed wire. Her nearness and the gentle scent of vanilla and leather often planted unbidden ideas in his brain.

Beyond that, however, he'd honestly enjoyed the quiet nights in front of the fireplace playing poker with her, learning about cattle, watching her read the Bible. She'd not tried once to cram her religion down his throat. Instead, he found her peace . . . calming.

Suddenly the stupid bouquet and the smirk on the jackass's face who delivered it loomed before him, reminding Dillon why he was in this establishment. Growling at the ridiculous ruminations regarding Audra, he thrust the empty glass out for a refill.

"Friend, we need a third. Care to play?"

Dillon glanced over at the table to his right. Two men, one a cowboy, one most likely a traveling salesman judging by his plaid suit, waited for his response. "Sure."

He settled in and gave the game all the attention he could muster. His thoughts wandered back and forth between the gal he'd just visited and how pretty Audra was the other day lunging that filly. Before the flower delivery.

"Dum dum da dum . . ."

Dillon clenched his jaw. A group of cowboys sauntered up to the bar, one of them humming "Here Comes the Bride." Though none of them looked at Dillon, he knew he was the object of their none-too-subtle humor.

He pushed a chip into the center of the table and waited to hear more. The cowboys didn't disappoint.

"That Winston has been holdin' out on us." Beers slid down the bar to waiting hands. "All the while he's been helping us bring girls in, when he coulda been shippin' *us* out to marry rich women."

The group laughed. "I reckon I'll go see him," another said, "and tell him I want to go off and marry a governor's daughter."

"Yeah, but the only thing about this, Sully, is you got to carry the bouquet."

The raucous laughter grated on Dillon's nerves.

"Mister, your bet."

Dillon blinked and slid another chip forward.

"Now, now, boys, the one thing you're missin'," Dillon recognized the man speaking now. *The cowboy who brought the flowers to the ranch.* "The one thing you're missin' is the type of woman who is willing to marry a total stranger." He cut his eyes at Dillon. "I reckon she ain't much different than Kit's girls."

Dillon knew what he had to do. He folded. Asked the salesman for a puff from his cigar, which the man gave, then he rose and strode over to the big mouth. The surrounding cowboys quieted down and backed off a few feet.

"What's your name?"

"Titus."

"Well, Titus, I want to be clear. Are you comparing my wife to a whore?"

"Mostly I'm just trying to figure out who wears the pants in your house."

Retorts ricocheted in Dillon's mind, but he skipped them and simply threw a ball pein hammer of a right hook. Titus went pin-wheeling backward, landing on and shattering a table. Men skittered out of the way as drinks, cards, and chips exploded in every direction. Titus scrambled clumsily back to his feet and he and Dillon traded several impressive punches. He hit the cowboy with one direct blow to the nose. The man stumbled but shook it off fast, ignoring the trickle of blood.

Face burning, arms heavy, knuckles bleeding, Dillon was still far from done and swung again at that bloody nose. This time, Titus didn't recover so fast. Not wasting the opportunity, Dillon stepped in to throw another punch, but sensed movement behind.

"We ride for the brand, mister," a voice said. "This is your wedding present from Fairbanks." White-hot pain fired up Dillon's kidney and he growled. Another fist slammed into the back of his head. Titus hit him in the gut. Suddenly, punches came from everywhere, falling on him like a black rain.

The world dissolved into darkness and pain.

CHAPTER 11

*A*udra knocked on Dillon's door. No answer. She tried again. After a moment, she pushed open the door, fully expecting to see him tangled in the sheets. His bed, however, was untouched. So he hadn't come home.

This time, she doubted he'd spent the night cleaning tack. Had he changed his mind about everything? Had he run off? Would she ever see him again?

The jangle of a wagon perked her ears up and she hurried to the porch. Bobby and Dale, still in their long johns, lounged in front of the bunkhouse, at nearly *eight* in the morning. Clearly, somehow they knew the boss wasn't at home. Well, she would be having words with them.

Winston drove up in his buggy, a bloody, black-and-blue Dillon by his side.

Her hand flew to her chest. "Good Lord, what happened to you?"

Dillon scowled at her, one eye swollen shut. "I was proving who wears the pants in this family."

"Did a pretty good job, too, till the other four jumped in,"

Winston said, winking at Audra. "But he defended your honor. As a good husband would. You can take him off my hands now, though. I've got to meet the stage. A couple of brides come in today."

Audra hurried to help Dillon down. He leaned heavily on her as they staggered inside. "Thank you, Uncle Winston," she called over her shoulder.

Audra bustled about the kitchen, gathering up the necessary supplies for tending to the swollen eye, raw knuckles, and fat lip. "Want to tell me what happened?"

"I do not."

Huffing at his ornery attitude, she sat down at the table with him and pulled his right hand forward. She'd rarely seen such a mess of bloody knuckles. "Does the other fella look this bad?"

"Fellas. And no."

She wiped away the blood as she talked. "How were you defending my honor?"

He fidgeted a moment before answering. "It was about your honor, but mine too." She freshened the alcohol on the rag and touched it to his skin, working a hiss from him. "Ouch."

"Sorry."

He watched her work for a moment before he spoke again. "I swear, I don't think I ever want to hear "Here Comes the Bride" again. Sort of lost its meaning for me."

"Oh," she said, drooping a little. "That again."

"That again. And comparing a woman who would take a mail-order husband to a . . ." Her hand poised to dab at his lips, he let the sentence die.

"Is that what they're saying about me?" Admittedly, it hurt. They both needed respect so badly, yet neither was getting it. She hadn't realized how much hinged on it. Sighing, she finished wiping his lip. "Did you prove it? Who wears the pants, I mean."

"To an extent."

She pulled away and folded her hands in her lap, perplexed as to how this had gone so awry. Admittedly, she hadn't for one second thought how this plan of hers might impact the poor *husband*. An idea came to her then. One that launched a billion butterflies. They had to start somewhere, though.

"Come with me." She took his hand and led him out to the porch. Facing him, and stepping in close, she said, "Bobby and Dale aren't even dressed yet. Somehow they knew you weren't here. They don't respect me. They only respect the fact that you're a man, I think. They sense, I don't know, that you're not—we're not . . ." She couldn't find the words. Dillon's eyes drilled into her, questioning, making her feel so foolish. "I think we have to be proxies for each other when it comes to running the ranch. And we have to show them that we're . . ."

"A team?"

"Yes . . . and no. Something more." She took a deep breath and rested her fists on his biceps. "Don't read too much into this."

"What?"

She put a hand on his neck, stood on her tip toes, and kissed him. Again, that amazing feeling flooded over her as her lips touched his, like standing in a warm summer rain. Then his arms encircled her, pinning her tight against him. He groaned in pain, but his mouth sought hers hungrily—caressing, craving. The kiss deepened, stealing her breath, making her head swim. Heat as if from an oven encircled her, and she tightened her grip on him. Dillon groaned again but not in pain, and the desire she heard made every inch of her—body and soul—cry out for him.

But suddenly terror sliced through the passion and she pulled away, shocked at herself. She fumbled blindly for the door. "Just for show," she whispered nonsensically and disappeared into the house like baying hounds were after her.

Dillon stood frozen on the porch. His mind stopped, but deep inside, far past physical reaction, he craved more of Audra, like a man dying of thirst in the desert. He'd kissed plenty of women, but this one little gal had the strangest effect on him. She was both terrifying and intoxicating.

She made him feel ten feet tall. Like a man.

He blinked and straightened up to his full height, twisting his head to scrutinize Bobby and Dale. Both men made a comical picture, slack-jawed, in their worn underwear. "You boys have work to do. Get to it." He grabbed the doorknob and narrowed his eyes at them. "I'll be along."

When Dillon's head cleared, he understood what Audra had done for him. But she hadn't faked her reaction. Just like he hadn't faked his. He wanted to say something, clarify what was happening between them, but she brushed past him headed for the door.

"Come on." She grabbed her shawl from the hook. "I want to give you something."

He followed her to the tack room. Grabbing the door to pull it closed, he spotted Bobby and Dale, finally saddling up for the morning's work. Mischievousness took hold. He winked at the boys with his good eye, and shut the door.

"I want you to use it."

Dillon walked over and brushed his hand across her father's saddle. "You don't have to do this. I can use any saddle."

She nodded. "I know you can. But you should use this one."

She started to go, but he caught her arm. He opened his mouth, eager to say something profound, something meaningful, but nothing at all came out. Too much to say and no idea what or how to say it.

"We've got to move the herd today. That is, if you can ride."

"I can ride."

"If you'll saddle Cookie for me, I'd appreciate it. I've got to change."

He dropped his hand. "Of course."

To occupy his mind and see just how sore he was, Dillon trotted Daisy around the barnyard. She was an old buckskin, a little deaf, a touch scrawny, but she was easy to ride. An intuitive horse with a smooth gait. His bruised ribs appreciated it. Maybe next time he'd see about a different mount—

His calm old nag exploded like a box of dynamite, kicking, screaming, twisting. Dillon went flying and landed in the dirt on his face, his mouth filling with earth, grass, and spilled oats. Behind him Daisy calmed a little, but still jerked, twisted, grumbled, and kicked once more as if trying to rid herself of a horsefly.

"Dillon, are you all right?"

Audra ran up to him as he peeled himself off the ground, brushing dirt and hay and other undesirable masses from his shirt and Wahmaker breeches. "Fine. Fine."

She frowned at him, her face an odd expression of terror and annoyance. "You nearly scared the life out of me." She shook her head, seemed to collect herself. "If you can't handle Daisy, I'll put you afoot."

Ignoring her, he wiped his mouth, spit once more, then strode toward his horse. "Shhh. Easy girl." Talking softly, gently, he eased up to Daisy, loosened her saddle and felt around underneath it. "Ouch." He snatched his hand out and examined his fingers. They were bleeding.

CHAPTER 12

"What the...?"

Dillon pulled the saddle off Daisy and threw it to the ground, upside down. He knelt and examined the exposed blanket.

"What is it, Dillon?"

He peered closely at something stuck in the weave. "Has anybody used this rig since your father died?"

"No."

He worked the shiny object loose from the blanket, but knew what it was before he had it free. He stood and handed it to her. "I don't know if someone was trying to kill your father, but they wanted to make sure he got thrown."

Audra stared at the dark brown piece of glass, turning it over and over in her hands.

Winston turned the piece of glass over and over in his hand, just as Audra had done. It did not, however, reveal its secret to him either. She would give her right arm to know. Had someone murdered her father?

Winston handed it back to her and sat down on the edge of his desk, eying her and Dillon sympathetically. "Without proof—"

"Proof? This piece of glass didn't walk into Pa's saddle."

"No, it certainly shows intent. Someone intended to harm your father. Harm is not murder. And furthermore, we have no idea who put the shard in his saddle. It could have been Fairbanks or any of those idiots who work for him. For that matter, it could have been Bobby or Dale."

Audra started to rise out of her chair to protest, but Dillon put a restraining hand in front of her. He leaned back in his chair. "He's right. We don't have any idea who put it there."

"Logic says Fairbanks," Winston wandered around the desk to his chair and sat. "But he could have had any of his boys do it. I'll go over the matter with Dent. I'm sure he'll open an investigation and ask around."

Dillon drummed his fingers on his thigh. "How dangerous do you think Fairbanks is? Do you think he would have tried to kill her father?"

Winston sighed, picked up a pencil, and tapped it on his blotter. "In his younger days, Fairbanks was a handful. Not afraid of the devil himself. Audra's pa put him in his place a time or two. I wouldn't say there was bad blood between them, but they weren't kissin' cousins, either. Then Fairbanks made some offers for the ranch over the years. But when Audra blossomed into such a beautiful young woman," he paused, choosing his words carefully, Audra guessed, "he got considerably more serious. The last time . . . they argued."

Dillon looked at her. "Which does Fairbanks want more? The ranch . . . or you?"

Audra hugged herself, nauseated by the thought of that

old man. He'd made his intentions quite clear since her father's death, to the point she'd slapped him at their last meeting.

Winston laid the pencil down and spoke softly. "He's come by to see you since your pa died, hasn't he?"

Her uncle seemed to already know the answer. Audra wanted to hide under the table. She felt undressed discussing this. "He . . . wants me. He said anyway he can get me."

Winston shook his head, his brow creasing under the burden. "I thought you might be safe with a man around, Audra. That was why I agreed to find you someone. Now I fear I've endangered two lives."

"I told him I wouldn't marry him if he was the last man on earth. But I didn't think he would hurt me or threaten my men, much less hurt Pa." She slid her gaze over to Dillon, "But what he said, the day we got married . . . now I'm not so sure."

"'You've just made things a whole lot harder than they had to be,'" Dillon repeated. "It was a threat."

Winston pointed at the glass. "If he did that to your pa, he's crazy. Be wary of him. Sit tight, stay away from him, and I'll get Dent started on the investigation."

CHAPTER 13

Audra pulled her horse up and raised her chin. Jess Fairbanks was riding toward her at a leisurely pace, as if they both had all the time in the world to dally. His white hair glistened beneath his black hat. Those ridiculous conchos on his belt and saddle reflected the early afternoon sun like mirrors. She regretted the decision to separate from Dillon to look for strays. Not that she was afraid of Jess, but she was far more suspicious of the man now than she'd ever been.

Did he murder her father? Her gut wrenched at the thought. She considered asking, but decided to hold back until she knew what he wanted. She started to ride toward him but paused. Waiting made her look more confident.

He rode up intimately close. "Afternoon, Audra." He challenged her with a bold stare.

She forced herself to stay put, hold his gaze, even though she was close enough to smell the whiskey on his breath, see the hunger in his eyes. "What do you want, Jess?"

"Where's your husband? You know, he never did tell me his name."

"No, but I'm sure you know it by now."

"Indeed, I do." He scanned the forest around them. "Is he nearby?"

"Hollering distance."

The old man smiled like the devil come to bargain for Faust's soul. "He's spent some time with Missy Galloway. She's a talker, that one. Spills everybody's secrets."

The news hit Audra hard. Her reaction perplexed her, but she hid it. "What's your point?"

He nudged his horse closer so his knee touched hers. "Missy tells me that your husband signed a prenuptial agreement. I'm no lawyer but I know Wyoming property law. Your husband owns your ranch just as much as you do." He swished his reins back and forth over the saddle horn. "Now, I asked myself, why would you try to buffalo him into believing he doesn't own it? Maybe 'cause you don't really want him to hang around." He sucked on his teeth, pondering. "Yep, I think you think he'll overstay his welcome if he knows that agreement isn't worth the paper it's written on."

Audra tired of the games. "What are you driving at, Jess?"

"I think I'll tell him that he owns one fine ranch, just as much as his new little wife does. Regardless of her lying, worthless attorney."

"Why? Why would you stick your nose in my business?"

"With a man around, I can use a different strategy. I'll bed you, girl, and I'll have your ranch. One way or the other."

A chill slithered down Audra's spine as the old man's eyes roamed over her. "Not in this lifetime."

He nudged his horse even closer and grabbed her face, gouging his fingers into her cheeks. "You brought another man into this. Now I can do whatever I want. When I get done with Dillon Pine, no cowboy this side of the Mississippi will be brave enough to work for you. You'll beg me to take you in and save your precious ranch."

Livid, Audra jerked away from him. "Did you kill my father?"

At first, shock registered on his face, then the evil, oily smile returned. "Only tried to hurt him, but I got lucky. I thought for sure I had you then. But, no, you had to go and get married," his lip curled into a sneer, "to a stranger. But I don't care whose son he is, I'll bury him to get what I want, Audra."

"You listen to me, Jess Fairbanks." She started backing her horse away from him. "Come near Dillon or my ranch and I'll bury you myself." When she felt far enough away, she spun Cookie and raced for home, the tears rolling down her cheeks.

Dillon let Daisy wander through the open pasture. Beneath a brilliant blue sky, the waving aspens and colorful pallet of dancing wildflowers eased his mind for a moment. He'd been distracted for days by that stupid piece of glass.

He agreed with Winston. It had not been put there as an outright attempt at murder. It was a warning. Dillon had a theory that Fairbanks had been pressuring Audra's father to sell the ranch and the suggestion went over about as well as Dillon would expect. The piece of glass implied another *no* would bring more trouble—worse trouble to the Diamond D.

A shot rang out. Daisy squealed, staggered, and collapsed. Dillon barely had an instant to draw his gun before he and the horse hit the ground. Climbing to his feet, he surveyed the tree line ready for a fight as the horse kicked, squealed once more, then fell silent.

Blood dribbled from a hole in her chest, just in front of

the saddle.

He waited, watching intently for several minutes. No more shots happened and he didn't see any movement.

Wait—there, a glint of light.

He dropped behind Daisy's body, his muscles loaded like a hair trigger, but nothing else happened. The minutes ticked by. Finally, he stood, doing one more careful scan of the trees. Nothing. Nodding, he knelt and unbuckled the saddle. Despite the long walk back, he wouldn't leave it here. He noted the bullet hole in the horse's chest. A foot higher and to the left and Dillon would be bleeding to death, his guts on fire from the bullet.

He patted the horse's neck. "Sorry, Daisy. But thank you."

CHAPTER 14

Her mind a whirling mess of raw emotions, Audra rode Cookie to the barn and dismounted . . . but she couldn't think what to do next. Should she find Dillon and warn him? Should she ride into town and tell Winston that Fairbanks confessed to killing her father?

He killed my father.

"Oh, God," she sobbed. Her knees buckled and she staggered over to the stall for support. He'd killed one man. No reason to think he wouldn't kill another.

Dillon couldn't stay. He had to leave.

She had done wrong by pulling him into this. By not seeing what was right in front of her—Jess was a killer. Her men hadn't run from her. They'd run from *him*.

Footsteps and the jangle of tack reached her. "Audra."

Dillon. She wiped her face and hurried outside to meet him. He was afoot and she knew that was a bad sign. He dropped the saddle as they both spoke simultaneously.

"What happened? Where's Daisy?"

"You've been crying. What's wrong?" He grabbed her

shoulders, his expression tender and full of intense concern. "You're pale as snow. What's the matter?"

It hit her like a lightning bolt.

Dillon mattered to her. Far more than her ranch. What did that mean? Could she—did she—*love* him? Clearly, if he had been visiting Missy Galloway, the feeling wasn't mutual. It didn't matter. She couldn't let anything happen to him.

"Get out." She nearly choked on the command, but he had to leave. "I'm done. I don't want to be marr—" her voice broke, but she fought to steady it. "I don't want to be married to you anymore."

Dillon's face fell. His lips moved, but no sound came out. Slowly, he released her.

She stepped back. "It was a terrible idea. It's not working. Get your things and leave. Take a horse. Any horse. I don't care." She couldn't stand the hurt in his eyes. *Why is he looking at me that way?*

She spun away from him and grabbed the stall door. "Go." She swallowed the tightness in her throat for one last word: "Please."

---

*D*illon stormed into his room and started shoving his belongings into his saddlebags. *Fine. I don't need the woman. Three years in prison would be a cakewalk compared to living with her, being taunted with flowers and wedding tunes...*

Wait a minute.

He chided himself for being ruled by wounded pride, and stopped packing to think. Something was going on here. He had to find the logic—the reason—in her transformation. So far, she hadn't been prone to any dramatic swings of emotion.

ASK ME TO MARRY YOU

What would make Audra suddenly decide to kick him out and end their marriage?

Had someone taken a shot at her, too?

No . . . he squeezed the shirt in his hand. The glint of light from the rider. Fairbanks's conchos.

Had he talked to Audra out there, while she was alone? Threatened her?

Dillon tried sliding the pieces of this puzzle into place.

Fairbanks was most likely the one who killed her father, whether by intention or accident. He wanted the ranch and Audra.

You've just made things a whole lot harder than they had to be.

By bringing a man into the picture? Audra had protection now? This was no simple matter of running off her hands. And she'd been pretty adamant about making sure Dillon gave the orders.

Which meant Dillon was the obstacle Fairbanks would have to remove.

Maybe this was a weak chain of reasoning, but it made sense. He couldn't think of anything else that would make her change her mind so suddenly. She was afraid for Dillon . . .

There was another possibility, of course. Was she afraid *of* Dillon? Of her feelings for him? Had he come to mean something to her? Would she rather see him leave than get hurt?

He didn't want to leave *her*.

He sat down hard on the bed. The realization that she had come to mean something to him felt like a mule kick to his gut. Oh, he wasn't in love or anything. Nah. He just liked her. He liked the sound of her voice, soft and hypnotic. He liked watching her ride, the way she joined with the horse in simple movement. He liked the way she'd held his hand and soothed his cuts.

He recalled the way she had walked into his jail cell. Her

stubborn chin lifted, shoulders back, she looked like a woman going into battle . . . and his heart had done a funny little flip. That wasn't love, though.

Then what was it?

Pressing a hand to his forehead, he groaned. What a tangled mess.

There was only one way to straighten it out—and keep Audra safe. Charge head-on for Fairbanks. He was the one strand in the knot keeping everything snarled.

CHAPTER 15

The Bar FB ranch house was an imposing white-washed, antebellum structure with two large columns supporting the front porches. Dillon rode straight to the hitching post, dismounted, and stomped up the steps. A lazy guard casually rose to his feet, clearly intending to stop Dillon with nothing but a hard look. Not wasting a moment, Dillon slugged the man, knocking him unconscious. The guard slithered to the floor with a fleshy thud and Dillon slipped inside the house.

He listened for a moment, picking up the muffled grumbling of Fairbanks from behind a closed door. "Well, here goes nothing," he whispered, and pushed into the drawing room.

Fairbanks and Titus spun to face the door. Both men went for their guns, but Dillon was faster and cleared leather first. While their eagerness to draw shocked him, staring into the barrel of his .44 quickly changed their fighting posture into acquiescence. They raised their empty hands.

"I just want to talk to you, Fairbanks." He eyed Titus, who clearly looked worried. "My bridesmaid, there, can leave."

Titus's jaw tightened, but Fairbanks dismissed him with a nod. "Go on. I don't believe the senator's son here has any intention of shooting us. He wouldn't do something like that to his father again."

Dillon's grip tightened on his gun. If Fairbanks knew, it wouldn't be long before the papers and everybody else knew, and his anonymity would disappear like smoke. He clamped his mouth shut, putting on a poker face. Titus walked past—glaring—but seemed to understand retreat was not optional.

"Titus, don't forget to tell Consuela I want chicken for dinner."

Titus paused, looked puzzled for an instant, then nodded. "Chicken? Yes, sir."

When the door closed, Dillon slipped his Colt back into its holster. "I have a question for you, Fairbanks."

"How did I find out who you are?"

"Nope. Did you kill Audra's father?"

The old man's beady, pale eyes widened, but he quickly tried to cover the response with a stoic mask. "Did she tell you that? It's a lie. His horse threw him. There were witnesses."

Dillon reached into his pocket and pulled out the piece of glass he'd found in Drysdale's saddle. "This is from a whiskey bottle." He tossed it to Fairbanks, who caught it out of reflex. "Now, the funny thing is, I happen to know whiskey. That is from the bottom of a bottle of Dunville's Three Crowns Whiskey. An Irish distillery. Somewhat rare. Very expensive." Dillon aimed a thumb at the bar beside Fairbanks where two Dunville bottles dominated the marble counter. "I doubt anyone else in Evergreen has even one bottle."

"What whiskey I prefer doesn't prove a thing."

"Maybe not, but it's just enough to give the sheriff cause to open an investigation. You want him poking around, asking questions?"

Fairbanks's face hardened, revealing his simmering rage. The rattlesnake was stirring, and Dillon was wary. "While he's asking questions, maybe you should ask your sweet little wife why she's lying to you about your rights."

"What are you talking about?"

"That prenuptial agreement isn't worth the paper it's written on. You're just as much legal owner of Diamond D Ranch as she is. Reckon why she tried to buffalo you?"

Dillon knew what Fairbanks was trying to do and it wouldn't work. "Is all this about your lust for land or Audra?"

Fairbanks took a long time to answer, his cold stare challenging and intense. When he finally spoke, his words dripped with arrogance. "I'm not a bad-looking man for my age. I've got a lot to offer Audra. I've told her time and time again she could keep her ranch. I'd help her run it and it would become bigger than her pa ever dreamed. All I wanted was more children."

"But she kept turning you down. You don't like to be turned down, do you, Fairbanks?"

"I always get what I want. Eventually. Then you came along. I saw the way she was lookin' at you in the wagon that day. I tried to be easy with you at first, just run you out of town as a laughingstock. But you wouldn't go."

"So you tried to shoot me."

"I don't know what you're talking about."

"The bigger question is how did you know getting Drysdale's horse to throw him would kill him?"

"I didn't. He was a big man, failing health. I just wanted to put him in bed for a while so's I could make things clear to his men. Him dyin' was just dumb luck."

"I've heard enough." Sheriff Hernandez stepped into the room, gun drawn. "You were right, Pine. He couldn't keep his mouth shut."

Fairbanks's eyes narrowed with fury. To his left, a door

Dillon hadn't noticed flew open and Titus leaped into the room, gun drawn. Fairbanks reached for his own. Dent and Dillon reacted. Guns roared four, five, six times. Smoke filled the room. Titus tumbled to the oriental carpet, dead, and silence like the grave settled with him.

Fortunately, the sheriff had taken the ranch hand, and Dillon had gone for Fairbanks. Fairbanks looked at his bloody shoulder and his eyes widened to full moons. His horror at his injury dawning on him, he let out a groan. Then his gaze landed on Titus, face down on the oriental rug, blood seeping from beneath him. Fairbanks screeched, a strange, wild sound, and flung his smoking .44 to the ground as if it were a hot coal. "He did it." He pointed at Titus. "He's the one who killed Drysdale." He clutched his arm. "It was all his idea. I just wanted the old fool laid up—not dead."

The sheriff stomped over to him. "Well, Titus can't exactly argue with you now, can he?" He shoved Fairbanks into a leather chair and glanced at the door Titus had burst through. "Consuela, bring me some towels! I got a man shot in here!"

Dillon, his nerves twitchy as telegraph wires in an electrical storm, heard a rustling from behind and spun. Audra and Winston stepped hesitantly into the room. "We heard it all," Winston said to the moaning Fairbanks. "And we'll testify against you."

Consuela burst from the kitchen and handed a stack of red-checked towels to Dent. The robust Mexican woman then made the sign of the cross and spit on Fairbanks, all in one smooth movement. Dillon got the idea it wasn't the first time the woman had done such. "I no more work here, Señor."

She stormed from the room, snatching off her apron as if it reviled her. Dent tossed the towels on the desk, keeping one to shove into Fairbanks's shoulder. The man grimaced, and hissed in pain.

"Quit your belly-aching. You're not gonna die," he pressed the old man's good hand to the towel, "but you will stand trial for murder, attempted murder, assault, and anything else I can come up with."

"When hell freezes over," Fairbanks whispered through clenched teeth.

Dent leaned in. "I'll get ya a blanket." He pulled the prisoner to his feet. "Pine, you want to help me get him to town?"

Dillon holstered his gun. "With pleasure."

"I'll tell." Fairbanks glared at Dillon. "I'll tell your father. I'll wire every newspaper in the country. The black sheep of the family brings another scandal down on his family."

Winston took a few more steps into the room. "Shut up, old man. Senator Pine's son is a hero. *I'll* wire every newspaper in the country."

"And so will I." Audra marched up to Fairbanks and looked him right in the eye. "And I'll make sure the papers know how you threatened my men . . . and how you tried to manhandle me."

CHAPTER 16

Audra sat on her front porch in the last rays of sunset, rocking, waiting for Dillon, though she had no way of knowing if he would come back. She'd told him to leave; she shouldn't expect him. Yet he hadn't left without getting Dent the evidence he needed to arrest Fairbanks for murder.

And he'd nearly been shot for his trouble.

She felt terrible. She owed him so much. Her insides twisted with regret and longing. What if she never saw him again? What if he dropped off Fairbanks and rode out of Wyoming?

"Oh, Pa," she whispered, "the ranch has never been this lonely. But I hope we'll get you justice."

The thought was of little comfort. Nothing would bring Pa back. Would anything bring back Dillon?

"I meddled, Lord. Just like Sarah and Abraham. They didn't wait on you. Neither did I. I rushed off half-cocked, thinking I'd found the answers. Now look where we are."

Restless, she rose and sauntered over to the porch post. She leaned a shoulder on it and eyed the new barn. Bigger and better than the one that had burned, the fresh lumber filled the air with pine. But she was back to square one as far as the ranch was concerned.

At least losing it would hurt less than losing Dillon.

She heard the fast clip-clop of a cantering horse and looked toward her gate. Audra's hand flew to her chest to keep her heart from beating out of her body.

She could feel his gaze long before she could see him clearly. Butterflies cavorting in her stomach, she meandered out to the hitching post and waited. He might not stay, but she would at least get a chance to say thank you . . . and good-bye.

Dillon rode to within a few feet of her and slid from the saddle, his hypnotic blue eyes stealing her will. He approached her, coming so close she could feel his breath on her face. She tried to slow her own breathing, to no avail. "I wasn't sure you'd come back. I was afraid I wouldn't get to say thank you."

"Audra," he raised his hands as if to grip her shoulders, but dropped them to his side. His throat worked for a moment, till finally he managed words that came out more like a plea. "Do you really want me to leave?"

What did the future look like if she said no? In a year, would he ride out and take the pieces of her heart with him? Would it just begin a long, painful goodbye? Regardless, she owed him the truth. "Dillon, I have to tell you something. I lied to you about our prenuptial agreement. It's worthless. You own this ranch with me."

"Why didn't you tell me?" He didn't sound surprised.

"I didn't want to share. I thought nothing in this world mattered more to me than the Diamond D. Then, when Fairbanks said he was going to go after you," she closed her eyes, sick over the impact of her greed, "and I'd put you in danger, I knew it wasn't true anymore."

He touched her cheek. "Audra, I don't want to leave

either. But I don't know what staying means." He took her hand in his. "I'll be honest, I don't feel like I'm married because I didn't get to court you." He pulled her hand to his chest and covered it with both of his.

When he didn't continue, she let the spark of hope ignite. "Are you saying you'd like to?"

"If you'll let me. I don't know exactly how it'll work, us being married and all, but I guess we can figure it out."

Audra swore she could feel her heart melting. If this wasn't love, she couldn't imagine how she'd stand under the pressure of the real thing. "Yes, Mr. Pine, you may call on your wife."

Grinning, Dillon gathered her up in his arms and kissed her gratefully, desperately. Audra felt lightheaded, as if his mere touch stole her senses like a heady drug. Slowly, deliberately, he pulled his body away from hers until, her face in his hands, only their lips touched. She tried to press in again, but he moved back, holding her shoulders.

"There's one thing." His lips twisted into a cocky grin, "when you ask me to marry you again, I want a preacher to do the honors."

"When *I* ask y—?" Audra bit down on the argument and decided, for once, to practice a little patience and obedience. She fluttered her eyelashes at him in a decidedly feminine manner. "Whatever you say, my husband."

Dillon's eyebrows rose and he'd never looked more pleased. "We just might be able to run this ranch together, after all."

She bit her bottom lip trying to hide the grin, but it wouldn't be denied. "We just might."

PART II

A PROPOSAL SO MAGICAL

A Proposal So Magical

Evergreen's sheriff, Dent Hernandez, has fallen in love and now actually has to do something about it or risk losing the woman he loves.

Once, the toughest lawman in the territory, Dent has been brought to his knees by love and he knows it's time to ask Amy to marry him. He has to make the proposal in a truly magical and courageous way. A handsome ghost from her past, though, has designs of his own on Amy.

Hunting outlaws was never this hard...

Proverbs 30:19

18 "There are three things that are too amazing for me,
four that I do not understand:
19 the way of an eagle in the sky,
the way of a snake on a rock,
the way of a ship on the high seas,
and the way of a man with a young woman.

CHAPTER 1

Amy Tate drifted around the empty schoolhouse, picking up slates and daydreaming about her handsome lawman, Dent Hernandez. He had finally settled into his role as Evergreen's interim sheriff, telling her just last night how much peace he was finding in the job. He didn't miss being a U.S. Marshal. He thought he could let the lies and betrayal of the past go and look ahead. To a future with her. And then he'd said, "I love you, Amy. You're healing me."

Her heart swelled with peace and joy. "Thank You, Lord," she whispered. "You've brought him so far. And I know You'll bring him all the way."

Mindful of her injured shoulder and the repugnant sling, she hugged the slates, trying not to powder her dress with chalk. Soon she would be *Mrs.* Dent Hernandez—though no actual date had been discussed yet. He hadn't even officially *asked*. They had just sort of *fallen* into planning their future. Not that he needed to drop to one knee or anything so showy, she supposed. They were engaged by a tacit agreement.

Surely that was good enough.

The lack of a formal request must be her fault. Dent wasn't pushing a date because Amy had said she wouldn't wear a wedding dress with her arm all but strapped to her side. She rotated her left shoulder. It pinched some still, but the muscle there was healing, enough that she could dress and do some chores without having to live in the sling all the time now. Soon she would cast it off for good and get on with her life.

She *was* almost whole again. In body and spirit. She wasn't afraid to be alone anymore. The nightmares were gone now, too. Dent was healing her as well.

One day soon, she'd wake up to his dark eyes, silky black hair, and handsome grin right beside her, and she would never be without him again—

The soft thud of a horse's hooves outside set to flight a thousand butterflies in her breast.

Dent came by often after school to escort her home. Giddy with joy and desire, she dropped the slates on a desk and rushed to the door.

Only, the young man who pushed it open as she reached out ... was not Dent.

---

*D*ent Hernandez, clutching his hat in his hands, walked almost on tiptoe down the aisle of the empty church. He couldn't see letting his boot heels disturb the quiet. A special quiet. Holy.

About halfway down, he stopped. Where was he going exactly? Hanging on the back wall, a large wooden cross, rugged, rough-sawed, about six feet tall, dominated the rustic sanctuary. He was a little intimidated by it, the sacrifice behind it, but not afraid of it.

He eyed the simple wooden pulpit Pastor Wills stood

ASK ME TO MARRY YOU

behind on Sundays. The man sure could rip loose with some heart-tugging sermons ... or maybe that was just how Dent was affected by them now.

He'd been feeling odd as of late. Over-the-moon for Amy, but dogged by self-doubts. What did he really have to offer her?

Drumming his fingers on the ring in his breast pocket, he decided to slip into the pew on his right. He wasn't even sure why he was here, but he had questions and thought Jesus might share some answers.

Not that he was exactly on a first name basis with the Lord, but Amy kept telling him Jesus was patient. When Dent was ready to surrender his heart, God would be waiting. She was fond of saying *He isn't going anywhere.*

"So, Lord—" He flinched, chagrined by his volume. He set his hat beside him and folded his hands. "Lord," he whispered, "I'm a flawed man. She's beautiful, smart, tough, the most patient woman I've ever known." He saw the faces of her children in the classroom. "But not just with them. With me. Sometimes I feel like I love her so much, I think I'd quit breathing if I lost her." He shook his head, again seeing the little puff of red wool as the bullet entered her shoulder.

Because of Dent, Ed Coker had nearly killed her. To add insult to injury, the slimy, murderous politician—the mayor of Evergreen—had gotten off. He and his attorney had argued all the evidence was *circumstantial* and Coker had walked free. At least he had walked on out of Evergreen.

"I don't have anything to bring to the table other than a reputation as a heavy-handed U.S. marshal, a gifted hangman, and an awkward town sheriff. I haven't caught the man who killed my pa. I couldn't get a conviction on the man who shot her. She deserves a whole lot more for a husband, Lord. A doctor or a lawyer." He slipped the simple gold band from his pocket to ponder it. "Not some two-bit lawman."

Disgusted with his dark past and its trail of bodies, he felt like tossing the thing across the room. "I'm not worthy of her love ... or Yours."

"You can't think like that, Dent."

Pastor Wills's voice startled Dent up from the pew and he spun like he was about to be fired upon. The old man waved his hands. "Sorry, I didn't mean to spook you." He motioned for Dent to sit back down as he sat across the aisle from him. "My apologies for eavesdropping, but I walked in and there you were. Seemed more respectful to quietly wait you out."

Dent felt his cheeks heat up. He'd been caught praying. He'd humiliated himself a lot of different ways over the years but this had to be the worst. "You could have walked out instead of listening."

"Honestly, I started to." Pastor Wills stared up at the cross, the corners of his eyes crinkling with concern. "But something you said stopped me." Slowly, he swung his gaze back to Dent. "You said she deserves more than a two-bit law man. And that you're not worthy of her love ... or God's. Dent," he shifted in his seat to face him, "First John 4:10 says 'Herein is love,'" emotion filled the pastor's voice. "'Not that *we* loved God, but that *He* loved us, and sent His Son to be the propitiation for our sins.'"

Propitiation? Not knowing the big word made Dent feel worse. "I-I don't understand."

Pastor Wills grinned kindly, like he was talking to a child. "Let me explain it in a different way. Though mankind was lost in sin—lost in darkness beyond description—that didn't change the fact that He loved us and He wasn't going to lose us. To break the curse of sin, to win us back, He had to die for us."

"How did His dying save anybody?"

"Sin entered the world through one man—Adam. And

one man—Jesus— overcame it. The ultimate sacrifice motivated by pure love."

Dent was utterly baffled by this idea of dying for humanity and thereby cutting the smooth path to Glory. He held his hands up like he was trying to guess the length of a fish, a very big one. "I can't—it's so big—the—the idea of what you're telling me."

"I know. I know. It's hard to understand. But, simply put, God loves us in spite of ourselves. He doesn't qualify us. He has no expectations of perfection. He loves us as we love our own children. At least that's the closest comparison I can give you. And like any good parent, God refused to just let the enemy come and snatch us away."

Pastor Wills stood and walked over to Dent. "Bear in mind, God sees us as who we can *become*, not who we are now. And, apparently, most of us were worth dying for. You are precious to Him, Dent." He grinned, lightening the mood. "And to Amy. You won't go wrong by putting a ring on her finger."

Embarrassed, Dent tucked the ring back into his pocket and stood, absently tapping the star on his vest. "You heard that part, too."

"Mmm-hmmm."

"I was thinking about making the request official this afternoon."

"One knee and all that?"

"Yes, sir."

Pastor slapped him on the shoulder. "I hope I helped to make it easier ... and anytime you want to talk about *God's* love, my door is open."

Dent shook the pastor's hand. "Thank you." As he walked back to the church entrance, one thing Pastor said stayed with him.

He sees as who we can become, not who we are now.

Dent found a tremendous amount of hope in the idea.

For an instant, Amy couldn't place the pale green eyes, curly caramel hair, and devastating smile. But then the memory of a gun firing into the air brought it all back in biting clarity.

The attack. The pawing, clutching hands, her dress tearing, exposing her shoulder ... and the deafening crack of a .38 fired overhead. Her attackers had run away and Jeremy, her savior, had lifted her to her feet.

Flooded with joy at the sight of the man who had saved her and become a dear friend, she jumped into his arms, holding in her injured wing. "Oh, my goodness! Jeremy!"

He wrapped her up tightly and spun her with equal enthusiasm. "Amy!"

Laughing, he twirled her around like a doll. She squeezed his neck, thrilled to see him. "Oh, how wonderful! What a surprise."

He kissed her on the forehead and set her down, but held on to her waist. "You are a sight for sore eyes."

"Oh, so are you. So are you." She caressed his cheek. "I can't believe you're here." The smile fell from her face as she stepped back. "What are you doing here?"

His dark eyebrows crashed in confusion. "Your father didn't mention me?"

"Mention you?"

"Yes. In the telegram about the books."

Amy was lost. "The last telegram I got from Father said they'd like to know more about Dent and how big our library is."

Disdain crossed his face, but he passed it in a flash. "You should have gotten a telegram about the books and that I would be arriving to help you set up the new library. You don't know anything about that?"

"Father and I have been asking for donations, but I had no idea anything had been collected."

"Hmmm." Jeremy rested his hands on his hips. "Well, I hate to tell you, young lady, but we have rounded up over five thousand books for this town's new library."

"Five *thousand*?" Amy was bowled over by the number. Evergreen finally had the inventory for a real, substantial library? Squealing like a fourth grader, she jumped up and hugged Jeremy again. He returned the hug—with relish, she thought—and kissed the top of her head, lingering this time.

Amy froze. Her familiarity and intimacy with her friend had crossed the line. She swallowed and stepped back, lifted his hands from her hips, but he instead clasped her fingers. His gentle gaze spoke volumes and her heart broke for him, but she had truth to speak. "Jeremy, I met someone here in Evergreen. My parents should have told you."

He ran his thumb over her fingers and nodded. "I know. They did tell me. They told me of your close call, as well." He glanced at her injury. "And maybe I shouldn't be here, but we were, I thought, close back in Ohio. You left in such a hurry, though—"

"I know. It was sudden. I'm sorry. But I couldn't sleep. I couldn't think." Amy turned away and hugged herself. "I was scared all the time, and you were confusing me. I was so grateful to you for saving me. I simply wasn't sure it was more than that. I needed to get away to think. To heal."

"It was never my intention to confuse you, Amy. I'm here now just as a friend."

"A friend?" She turned back to him. "Long way to come just to see a friend."

He shrugged and slid his hands into his pockets. "Truthfully? I was injured in the line of duty a month ago—"

"Oh, no, are you all right?"

"Fine. A concussion, but I'm on temporary leave. Your father asked me to escort your shipment. He's paying me for the security work."

"My books need a bodyguard?"

Jeremy chuckled and scratched his nose. "Your parents sent all your jewelry, as well. I understand your collection is quite valuable. Your mother also shipped some furniture. They filled an entire car for you."

Amy frowned. Things. Her parents could always be counted on to send *things*, but they had not agreed to come if there was to be a wedding. Regardless ...

She ambled back over to Jeremy and smiled. "I am doubly-blessed then. To receive such a wonderful shipment watched over by someone I adore."

He touched her cheek. "Honestly, I had forgotten how pretty you are."

A man clearing his voice at the door startled Amy and she jumped away from Jeremy. Dent stood in the door—her tall, handsome, rugged sheriff—and her heart raced at the sight of him. The troubled, disapproving crease in his forehead said he had some serious questions about the scene before him.

CHAPTER 2

Dent never knew what he might wander into when he stopped by the school. A little girl practicing her part as the Statue of Liberty. A little boy being admonished to *not ever* bring snakes to class again. A teenage girl sobbing into Amy's shoulder, lamenting a break-up.

He was *not* prepared for the sight of a strange young man in a tailored suit caressing her cheek. It sent him reeling. As he dragged his hat from his head, a sick feeling exploded in his gut. He knew he wouldn't be dragging the ring out today. Worse, he became aware of his worn vest, scuffed boots, and shaggy, black hair in need of a trim.

"Dent, perfect timing." Amy hurried over to him and took his hand. "I need you to meet Jeremy." She dragged him back to her friend. "He is the off-duty policeman who came to my rescue when I—" even now she still stumbled when speaking of it— "when I was attacked. He chased the men away."

The sick feeling waned, but didn't disappear altogether. Still, relief was there and Dent focused on it, offering the tall stranger his hand. "I don't have the words to tell you how grateful I am. Thank you." They shook, but this *old friend* broke the grip rather quickly, Dent noted.

"It was my pleasure," Jeremy said with a nod to Amy. "And I would certainly do it again."

Yes, yes, he would, Dent agreed, watching Jeremy's eyes soften as he gazed at Amy. The knife of jealousy twisting again, he tried to force it away and think like a lawman. "So what brings you to Evergreen?"

"Oh, that's the best part, Dent." Amy beamed as she clutched his arm. "He escorted a shipment of books here for the library."

"That's good news. The town's wanted a library forever."

"Guess how many books?" Amy quivered with excitement. "Guess."

Dent hated guessing games. "A thousand."

"Five. Five *thousand* new books."

"That's a mighty big lot. Must be pretty valuable to need security."

"I was just telling Amy, her parents also sent her collection of jewelry. It's quite valuable. But honestly," he shrugged a shoulder, "Amy's father was just trying to help out a low-paid police officer who's on medical leave."

"Medical leave, huh?"

"Mild concussion. Nothing serious. Department regulations. But I'm off for a month."

Dent tried to keep the relaxed look on his face, but felt the sneer fighting for freedom. "A whole month."

"Oh, Dent isn't it too good to be true? We'll have a fine library established almost overnight." She spun back to Jeremy and clutched his arm. "I can't wait to get started. Join Dent and me for dinner tonight and we can talk about it."

"I'd love to. Sheriff, I borrowed the hotel owner's surrey to get out here and need to return it. Would you mind giving me a lift to dinner, since I don't know my way around town yet?"

The sick feeling, mixed with a heavy dose of annoyance, churned in Dent's stomach. "My pleasure."

"Wonderful. I'll see you about ...?"

"Six," Amy said.

"Six," Jeremy repeated to Dent. "You'll pick me up a few minutes before, Sheriff?"

Not sure he could hide his sour mood, Dent merely nodded. Jeremy excused himself and slipped back outside. When the door closed, a delicate, warm hand slipped into Dent's. Trying to recover his good mood, he dropped his hat onto her head. "Funny how it always looks better on you."

Waves of long, pretty, auburn hair tumbled down her shoulders. Behind her spectacles, her mesmerizing blue eyes glowed with a hypnotic warmth. Dent fell under their spell, letting this sick feeling drown under a wave of desire. She looked at him sometimes like he was the greatest thing since sunlight.

"You handled that well." A half-grin playing on her lips, she reached up and straightened the hat.

"What?"

"Oh, goodness, Dent, if your face was any stiffer, it would shatter." Opening up the grin, she leaned into him. "You don't have a thing to worry about." She rose on her tiptoes, lifted her face to him, and closed her eyes.

If she wasn't the cutest thing ... he kissed her, followed her for another when she started to pull away. Laughing, she changed direction and wrapped her arm around his neck. He gave her another innocent peck, but somehow it transformed into a long, deep kiss. He lost himself in the heat of her mouth, the feel of her curves against him, the sound of her breathing. His hands slid from her ribs to her back, to the curve of her waist.

"Never fails to amaze me what you do to me," he whispered against her throat. She yielded to him, setting fires in his muscles. He nibbled on her ear lobe. "Amy, save me from myself." He dragged his lips down her jaw to her mouth. "The water is gettin' deep."

She took a deep breath and slid her fingers up, covering his mouth. Capping the bottle. Eyes closed, he rested his forehead on hers and let sanity seep back into him. They were both breathing as if they'd run a mile.

She shook her head. "You keep kissing me like that, we might both drown."

"Promise?"

She took another deep breath, as if for strength, and stepped out of his arms. "There are particular things that should be in place first." Her eyes flashed him a challenge.

Like a proposal. And, boy, wasn't the idea tempting? The ring beckoned to him, but the appearance of *Jeremy* had him off-balance. Dent plucked his hat from her, and dropped it on his own head. "There certainly are." He took her hand in his. "Long as that Jeremy fella doesn't cause any problems, maybe I'll get around to those particulars."

She squeezed his hand. "Then you'd better start planning."

---

*B*ecause a good woman had raised him right, Dent had allowed himself to be hornswoggled into giving this Jeremy a ride to Amy's.

Nobody said it had to be a comfortable ride.

Dent rode up to the front of the hotel astride his sorrel Ginger. He held the reins to a swaybacked piebald gelding who didn't leave the pasture much. Consequently, the activity on Evergreen's main street—not to mention the strange surroundings—had the horse, known as Baldy, two-stepping at the slightest noise.

The gelding would calm down quick, but Jeremy would have an interesting few minutes in the saddle. If he could stay in the saddle. Dent guessed most police officers from Swanton weren't too familiar with horseback riding.

He was about to dismount when Jeremy walked out on to the hotel's porch, a new derby in his hand. "You don't have a buggy?"

Dent settled his rear end back into the saddle. "I do, but it's out at my ranch. I take it you don't ride?"

"No, I ride." He double-timed down the steps. "It's just this boy looks like he's on his last leg." He took the reins from Dent and ran a hand over Baldy, causing the horse to neigh and side-step away from the touch. Jeremy calmed him with some soft words and swung up.

As Dent had predicted, Baldy's eyes rolled back, he tossed his head about, grumbling in protest, and danced at the hitching post like snakes were slithering at his feet. Hiding his amusement behind a gloved fist, Dent leaned forward and rested an elbow on his saddle horn. "Pretty energetic for his last leg."

Jeremy pulled the horse's left rein in tight, working him into a circle. The horse whirled several times, but finally started calming. "Whoa, boy, whoa," he commanded in a firm, but soothing tone. After a moment, the gelding came to a standstill and he loosened the reins.

Jeremy had brought the old boy under control with skill and confidence. Dent would give credit where credit was due. "You *can* ride."

Jeremy didn't look at him. Instead, he responded by backing Baldy out to the street. "I'm ready if you are."

Dent didn't miss the abrupt tone. He nudged Ginger away

from the post and the two horses fell into step down the street.

"Is that how you treat all your visitors in Evergreen? Put them on unruly horses too old to ride?"

Dent didn't bite at the acidic comment. "Baldy's a good horse. Once he's calm."

Jeremy chuckled, a bitter sound, then hit Dent with a baleful glare. "I know about you. This won't be a cakewalk. I won't just let her go. Especially with you."

Dent's mouth just about fell open over the brazen comments, but anger surged ahead of the shock. He was sorely tempted to reach over and snatch Jeremy out of the saddle, but right here in the middle of Main Street wasn't the place. He held his tongue, almost biting it off, till they had ridden past the busiest section of town.

"Friend, you are dangerously close to exhausting my patience. Explain yourself."

Jeremy's lip curled. *"Dangerously close.* Violence is your bailiwick. You got Ben Hayes killed and Amy shot. I've come to get her away from you before you get her killed."

Dent had never in his life beat anyone over a woman, but there was a first time for everything. "Mister—" It occurred to him he didn't know the man's last name and he did not want to be on a first-name basis with him.

"Dillard."

"Well, Mr. Dillard," Dent reined up, and turned in the saddle to look the swaggering fool right in the eye. "Whether Amy stays with me or goes with you will be her choice. Bear in mind, *I* won't just let her go, either. We have an understanding at the moment, and I am going to ask her to marry me."

"Going to ask. You're not engaged yet."

"I said we have an understanding."

"Which, as *I* said, is not engaged."

"It's the same thing. And I can tell you her heart is steadfast."

"Maybe. I would argue she hasn't had the right information to make the proper choices."

Well, this is a heck of a note.

The man had all but slapped Dent in the face and said he was going to steal his girl. He had no experience for dealing with this type of situation so he drew on what he did know. Since violence did not seem the gentlemanly option, as it would prove the man's point, he decided to issue a warning first—a warning he would be happy to act upon. "I am not in the habit of letting folks waltz into my life and take what is mine. Not without a fight."

Dillard smiled. An oily, dark thing that made Dent clench his fingers into a tight fist. "I won't *take* her. She'll come with me willingly."

CHAPTER 3

Dent and Amy ambled arm-in-arm down the street. Sunset was coming on quick, the bugs were buzzing around them, and the crickets started up their serenade for the spring evening. Dinner had been a long and painful affair. Dent had done his best not to reveal a desire to snap Jeremy Dillard's neck, but every time the man leaned into Amy and the two shared a private joke, his gut had twisted with jealousy.

"You were awfully quiet during dinner tonight." Amy said, plucking a June bug from his sleeve. "Is something wrong? Is it Jeremy?"

Could he lose her? Was Dillard right? Had she chosen Dent out of a lack of ... options? "You want to tell me about him?"

"I told you not to worry about him. I have given you my heart. Don't you believe that?"

Did he? He slid an arm around her. She felt as natural beside him as the air in his lungs. Her lilac gown, fitted snuggly to her curves and cut just a little low, had about knocked him off his feet. To top it all off, she smelled like a bouquet of roses. Even that darn sling didn't take the shine off her. "I guess I'm just a little ... stunned that I have captured a girl as special as you."

She poked him playfully in the ribs. "I think you're pretty special, too, Sheriff." She shoved her glasses up on her nose and studied him, like she was trying to figure out the perfect thing to say. "I love you to death. Truly, madly, deeply. How can you doubt me?"

He hung his head, pondering the question, then stopped walking. "He's got a lot to offer you." He turned to her and gently clutched her shoulders. "He makes more money than I do. He's educated—"

She pressed her hand to his lips. "Stop. Everything I want in a man is standing right in front of me. If Jeremy had been the man for me, I wouldn't have left Swanton. God brought me to you."

"Why, Amy? Why do you love me?"

"How much time do you have?"

His expression softened with the joke and he cupped her cheek.

She covered his hand with hers. "You're the bravest, most honorable man I've ever known. You're wise, noble, humble. You make me feel safe and warm and loved. Need I go on?"

"I was going to hang one of your students."

"No, you weren't. That's why you let him ride out. You gave Israel a second chance."

Dent sighed and stared up at the emerging stars. "I don't know what I did. But, you're right, I couldn't hang him." He scrubbed his face, weary of second-guessing that one decision. "What if he goes bad like his pa? Kills someone."

"He won't." The conviction of her belief drenched the statement. "Not Israel. He's away from his father now. He'll make something of himself. And that one choice showed me your heart more than anything else you've ever done. No one could make me happier, Dent. I'm *meant* for you. No one else."

"Dillard wants to argue that point."

"I know."

*A*nd it didn't matter a wit to Amy. She hooked her arms around Dent's elbow and the two started walking again. She could enjoy Jeremy's company while they worked on the library, which right now consisted of one room in the new town hall. She would have to do the work after school and on the weekends, which would cut into her time with Dent—something that wouldn't thrill him—but the sooner the project was complete, the sooner Jeremy would be gone.

She gazed up at her handsome sheriff, his white shirt glowing against his tanned, clean-shaven face, one rebellious sprig of dark hair trailing down his cheek. No, he was not fancy, or wealthy, or college educated, but he was wise, steady, and *hers*. She hungered for him in a way she never had for any other man. She almost told him so, but such information, one could argue, would lead only to trouble. She bit down a secret smile. They were both struggling enough as it was.

Laughter and fiddles drifted to them on the breeze and a moment later they could see lanterns for the spring dance glowing up ahead in the twilight, beckoning to them. They approached the teeming town square, where she thought Evergreen's entire population was milling around, eating scrumptious desserts, or dancing happily to a boisterous version of *Maggie's Schottische*.

"Oh, let's dance, Dent." Giddy from the spring weather, the surprise of seeing an old friend, the gift of all those books, and the intoxicating nearness of the love of her life,

ASK ME TO MARRY YOU

Amy pulled him forward. She wanted to spin and twirl and hold her sheriff close.

"No, I'm sorry." He dug his feet in. "I don't dance."

She tugged, thinking he was joking. "Oh, come on."

"No, really." He disentangled himself from her, but held her fingers lightly. "I really don't know how. I never learned."

"Then I'll teach you." She gripped his hand and pulled.

"No, I really don't—"

She tugged again, but realized he was quite serious. "You won't dance with me?"

"I told you I don't know how."

"And I told you I can teach you."

Dent's eyes darted around at the crowd. "No, maybe another time."

Amy's spirits sagged. She loved to dance. One of the few non-bookwormish things she enjoyed, to her mother's dismay and her father's delight. "Do you mean to tell me a former U.S. marshal who's been shot three times and stabbed five, slept too often on the ground in the cold, and nearly starved to death once, is afraid of looking silly to the people of Evergreen?"

The quote was an old joke between them, but her beloved didn't crack a smile. "I have no rhythm. It's that simple. I could learn, I suppose, but not here toni—"

Something cut off his words as his gaze shot past her. She followed his line of sight. Jeremy waved at them, straight, white teeth gleaming, and pushed through a group of young people. Amy adjusted her glasses. She had to admit he looked rather dashing in a dark, tailored suit and polished brogans. He'd even made time to trim his caramel hair which stopped now at the very edge of his collar.

Jeremy *was* handsome, but he was *not* her sheriff.

"Dent, Amy," he greeted them on approach.

"I thought you said you weren't up for the dance." She allowed him to greet her with a kiss on the cheek.

"I got back to my room, comfortably full from your dinner, and then I heard the fiddles."

"And you just had to come dance?"

"I did. I did." He passed a quick glance over Dent then to Amy. "I see you're not dancing. Would you take a turn with me then?"

She sucked in a breath. There was no way to say no without sounding rude, no way to say yes without exacerbating Dent's fears. But she so wanted to dance.

Jeremy extended his hand ...

Dent wouldn't be intimidated. He was still walking on air from all of Amy's praises and his confidence had soared. He released his hold on her. "Go ahead. I don't mind."

Confusion flitted over Amy's face, but she recovered quickly. "All right." She took Dillard's hand and the two drifted off toward the swirling crowd. But not before Dillard spared Dent a triumphant glare over the top of her head.

Dillon Pine wandered up just then, scratching his jaw. Dubbed Evergreen's mail-order *groom* because he had married Audra Drysdale to get out of jail, he was now in the curious position of *courting* his wife. He and Dent had become good friends over the last few months, swapping ranching tips and weekend deputy shifts.

"That man," Dillon motioned after Jeremy, "he's the one who rescued Amy?"

"Yep." The grapevine in a small town moved faster than fire on a dry prairie.

Amy was laughing and swirling—a picture of sheer joy—as Dillard guided her with confidence. He was light on his feet. Dent's mood sagged a little and he wanted to talk about something else. "So, how goes it with you and Audra?"

"It is a strange circumstance I find myself in, Dent. I'm in love with my wife and I'm having to court her." He rubbed his neck, as if the muscles there stored the tension from his entire body. "It makes for some interesting evenings."

Dent was familiar with the problem. Leaving Amy every night to return either to a cot at the Sheriff's office or the cold, lonely ranch was not ideal. But Dillon—he and Audra were married. "If it's going well, what are you waiting on?"

Long and lean like Dent, but fair-haired and heavier built, Dillon tilted his head and sighed. "Her. It's hard to explain, but you know how I got here. An arranged marriage, of all things. I want her to be sure. When *she* comes to me, I'll know."

Dent could see the wisdom in that approach, and the challenge. He rubbed the taut muscles in his own neck. Of course, he hadn't gotten that far yet. First he had to ask Amy to marry him. Until Dillard arrived, he had thought her *yes* was a foregone conclusion. Watching them out there now, he began to have doubts again.

Dillon studied the dancing couple and crossed his arms, a skeptical dip in his brow. "I'm a royal flop when it comes to reading a woman's mind, but I can read his. He's a wolf on the prowl."

"Said as much."

"He did? Hmmm ..."

Dent wasn't sure if Dillon sounded confused or impressed. "I figured I shouldn't act jealous. To my way of thinking, that gives him the upperhand."

"Sheriff," little Audra Drysdale—er, Pine—slipped up beside Dillon and hooked his arm. A pretty thing, she was small, petite, and one of the best cowboys Dent had ever seen. Her marriage to Dillon had saved her ranch and put a murderin' neighbor behind bars. He had quite a lot of respect for these two, but couldn't imagine the oddity of their situation. She *tsked* at him. "What you should worry about is how *Amy* sees things. It's her opinion that matters, not that fella's."

"You sayin' I should be jealous?"

"I'm saying every woman wants to know her man is a *little* jealous. The trick is don't overdo it or you'll look like an insecure fool."

With effort, Dent refrained from passing a frustrated hand over his face. This romantic *dance* was becoming too complicated. "I'm not jealous."

Audra shook her head. "No. Why would you be jealous of a tall, handsome stranger whose teeth are white enough to light up a room? And he sure likes showing them to Amy."

Dent clenched his fingers, eager to disagree. But she was right. Dillard was clearly enjoying spinning Amy around the floor. Holding her.

Dent wanted to kick himself. If he had just been willing to dance with the woman—but he had no idea how to and wouldn't risk that humiliation ever again.

CHAPTER 4

Cigar smoke hung heavy in the air over the spring dance. The musicians sweated as their fingers plucked and strummed. Friendly faces greeted Amy with enthusiastic nods as she swirled and dipped with Jeremy. Oh, how she missed dancing, though she would have given anything to be in Dent's arms instead. She knew the game Jeremy was playing. He could pour out all the charm he liked. Her heart was with the brooding sheriff over there on the side.

"Let's talk about books," he suggested, subtly moving her to the other side of the dance floor.

"Oh, yes, let's."

"The shipment is still sitting at the depot. I'll have them moved to wherever you say tomorrow."

"There's a room in the new courthouse waiting for them. I won't be able to get there until about two or so, but you could start an inventory and I'll assign the Dewey decimal numbers."

"Already done. Every book in the collection was tracked, catalogued, assigned its number, and put in its proper place.

All we have to do is unpack them. Your father even had library cards inserted in the backs of the books."

Amy was ecstatic. "That cuts down our work significantly. I thought we'd be working on this for a month. We should be able to have the library up and running in a matter of days."

"Yes, we'll make quick work of it. Sadly."

Amy didn't meet his gaze. While she was delighted at the new library and her father's generosity, she felt crowded by Jeremy, downright pressured. Why did he have to show up now? She couldn't let him get the wrong idea. "Jeremy ..." she adjusted her glasses using her bad arm and was pleased there was no twinge of pain. "I'm so glad you brought me the books and my jewelry, I truly am ... "

"But?"

She missed a step and they laughed. "I'm sorry. Was that your foot?"

He squeezed her hand. "I'll not complain." The good humor faded from his face. "All joking aside, Amy, I have to ask. With his penchant for violence—well, what in the world are you thinking?"

"That's a rather impertinent question, Jeremy."

"He seems to attract trouble and you've been in the middle of it twice now. Forgive me for saying so, but you're lucky to be alive, no thanks to him."

Amy took a deep breath to buy a moment to think before she responded. And a thought did come to her. "Jeremy, I realize you saw me at my worst. I was broken, afraid, confused. Needy." She let the word settle before continuing. "God is good. I've healed from all that and I'm even stronger than I was before. Dent has been a huge part of my recovery. You wouldn't know that because you didn't know me before the attack. I'm a grown, intelligent woman, and I can make my own decisions."

"I can see that."

They danced a few minutes in a tense silence. Amy didn't want to leave on an unpleasant note, especially since they had to work together on the library. Before she could find a way to bridge the gap, however, he spoke again.

"You have changed, grown. Perhaps you should look at Dent *and* me with fresh eyes. I came because I wanted to see you again. Not a day has gone by that I didn't think of you. My feelings are the same, Amy. Now I won't mention them again. If your affections toward me haven't changed by the time the library is ready, I'll kiss you goodbye and return to Swanton. Does that sound reasonable?"

Agreeing would bring peace between them and in a few weeks, he would be gone. "Yes. I think you'll be disappointed with the final result, but yes."

CHAPTER 5

*A*my stepped into the room that would soon be Evergreen's new library. The musty scent of books and fresh lumber wafted over her. She took in the chaos of pine shipping crates strewn about the large room, tables with books stacked willy-nilly on them, half-stocked rows of shelves, and Jeremy, arms full of books, walking from one bookcase to the other, setting them in their new homes.

She turned to Doc Woodruff, the grizzled, wise town physician, and—due to Coker's departure—the interim mayor now. "Look how much he's gotten done today."

"Pretty impressive." Scratching his chin, he stepped with her into the room.

"Jeremy, I can't believe how much you've accomplished."

He set an armload of books down and approached her, brushing the dust from his hands. "I have been a busy man. It keeps my mind occupied tracing down all those Dewey decimals."

Amy chose to ignore the subtle hint and motioned to Doc. "I'd like you to meet Doctor Henry Woodruff."

The two shook. "Nice to meet you, son." Doc surveyed the room again. "This is a mighty lot of books. We are going to have one fine library. We'll be the envy of every town in Wyoming. All because of our school teacher here and her friends. Thank you for helping."

"Ah, Amy knows I'd do anything for her. Setting up a library doesn't seem like hard work at all."

A troubled crease grooved Doc's brow. "Yes, I suppose we'd *all* do just about anything for her." He patted her on the shoulder. "She is a treasure to the town."

"Absolutely," Jeremy agreed, being too pointed with his gaze. "Priceless."

"Uh, well," Doc pulled out his pocket watch and checked the time. "I've got an appointment at my office. Amy, I'll send Dent by in a bit to escort you to dinner."

"Oh, about that," Amy waved a hand at the library, "I should have let you and Susan know sooner. I need to be here to do my part. We'll be working till about seven or so probably every night for the next few weeks." She shifted to Jeremy. "I've got papers to grade tonight. I can't stay past that."

"Well, I've put in a long day." He picked up his stack of books again. "Why don't we just go to six and then have dinner."

"Fine idea," Doc interjected. "I'll have Dent bring dinner for all three of you."

Amy bit her bottom lip to hide her appreciation of the suggestion and nodded. "That's a lovely idea."

"You'd best watch him, Dent." Doc motioned at him with a forkful of chicken. "He's after your girl."

The doc looked at his wife sitting at the other end of the dinner table. "Didn't you say you agree, Susan?"

"Amy told me he said some things regarding such, but she put him in his place."

The news brought Dent a little relief, but annoyed him at the same time. The man was forward, to say the least. Admittedly troubled, Dent flipped a chair around and settled into it, resting his arms on the cross beam. A quick, comfortable way to sit, since he was only picking up food, not joining the doctor and his wife. "You think I don't have anything to worry about then?"

Glass of buttermilk at her lips, Susan paused. "I didn't say that." She finished her sip and considered his question. "Until she says yes and has a ring on her finger, Dent, I don't think you should consider the competition over."

Competition? How had this dang-near perfect relationship with Amy suddenly gotten so convoluted? If she wasn't interested in Dillard—he decided to ask his question out loud. "If she has no interest, no feelings for this Dillard, what do I have to worry about?"

Doc snorted and Susan shot him a glare, her chubby, sweet face flushing. "Don't gloat, doctor. Just because you've been out of the game for forty years." She softened her voice for Dent. "No woman wants to feel as if she's being taken for granted. Make sure she knows you appreciate her, Dent. That way, he can't *cloud* her vision."

"I thought I was doing a pretty good job on that front." Maybe not if everyone in town was advising him to—

"Fight." Doc said flatly. "Don't take her for granted. Don't take him for granted."

A mild curse slipped through Dent's mind, but he did not say it aloud. That was progress for him.

"Dent, it's none of my business, I suppose," Susan laid her

fork down, "but did you have anything *grand* planned for when you ask her to marry you? Something magical?" Her hard gaze suggested he'd better say yes.

Dent felt like an elk staring down the barrel of a rifle. *Grand? Magical? In Evergreen?* "Not really. I mean, I almost asked her in the schoolhouse, but ... no, why? Should I?"

Susan's sympathetic expression made Dent feel like an idiot. She rose from the table and dropped her napkin in her plate. I"ll pack some dinner for you and Amy."

"And Dillard," he growled. "He's there, too."

She paused, shooting Doc an uneasy glance. "Yes, of course."

Of course.

Maybe he could take Amy to Cheyenne. A nice, candlelit dinner in a high-tone restaurant would be magical, wouldn't it?

Dent switched the picnic basket from his right hand to his left as he jumped up on the boardwalk. No, that wouldn't do. Not for Amy. Tipping his hat and nodding at a few passers-by, he scowled inwardly. Susan was right. Somehow Dent had to think of something special to dress up his proposal.

But what? He scanned the quaint, clean town of Evergreen, the streets almost deserted now in the settling twilight. Quaint, clean, and boring.

He used to despise this town for those very traits. Once upon a time he had been a man with warrants to serve, criminals to hang. No close attachments. No romantic entanglements. In his selfishness, his life had been simple. He did miss that.

Huffing in disgust, he crossed the street to the town hall. In the foyer, he heard Amy's rich, clear laughter, entwined, unfortunately, with a deep, throaty chuckle.

Dillard.

Dent softened his footfalls and approached the door to the library, a room just off the main alcove. He spotted the two, Amy on her knees digging into a box, and Dillard stocking a shelf with an armload of books. His jacket was draped over a nearby chair. He looked too comfortable, too natural, in the setting and that tweaked Dent like a mosquito bite.

"I don't know why you'd think that, Jeremy," Amy was saying. "I'm sure there are a lot of women in Evergreen who would love Bronte. She's not too high brow for us."

"You know, that sheriff of yours," he tapped the books into line and turned to her. "He does remind me of Heathcliff."

"Nonsense." She handed him two more books. "You just don't know him well, that's all. There's nothing dark and brooding about him." She frowned for an instant. "At least not anymore."

Dillard also slid those books onto the shelf, but paused with his hand on the collection. "Do you really believe that? A man with his kind of past ..." He swung around to her. "Amy, men like that don't just wash off the stink of death."

Amy stared into the box. Dent could tell she was struggling for a response. He started to respond for her, defend himself, when she tossed her auburn braid over her shoulder and lifted her chin. "You're wrong about him, Jeremy."

Buoyed by her support, Dent marched into the room. "Wrong about what?" Dillard and Amy looked startled by his arrival, even a little guilty—or at least she did.

But Amy wiped off the expression and replaced it with a

warm smile as she climbed to her feet. "Dent, I hope you've got dinner there. I'm starving."

He lifted the basket. "Susan loaded us up."

She hurried over to him, kissed his cheek, and took the meal from him. "It smells like fried chicken."

"Biscuits, potato salad, and green beans, too." Pretty much feeling like the cock of the walk now, Dent allowed a half-smile for the other man in the room. "Dillard."

He responded with a smile as warm as a rattlesnake's. "Sheriff."

Amy set the basket on the large table in the center of the room, which was mostly covered with boxes and books. Dent stepped in and cleared a few things out of the way to expand their eating area.

Dillard meandered to the food, peering over Amy's shoulder. "I do enjoy a fried chicken leg."

Obliging the subtle request, she snapped open a red checked napkin, picked up a chicken leg with it, and handed him the snack. "I can promise you, you've had none better than Susan's."

Amy and Dent unpacked the plates and together dished food on them. He noted with satisfaction how easy it was to work with her. They had a natural rhythm together. So far, Dillard hadn't been able to disrupt it.

Munching on the chicken leg, the man wandered the room, eying the paintings on the walls. The collection of art was random as far as Dent knew. One of President Hayes. One of Lincoln. A photograph of Evergreen when only two buildings comprised her main street.

"Sheriff, how many men have you hanged?"

Amy gasped. "Jeremy, that is not—"

"It's all right, Amy." Dent straightened up. "Eighteen." He wouldn't run from his past. Especially if this jackass was doing the chasing. "And I've killed twenty-two in attempts to arrest them."

"I'm a police officer, too." Dillard matched Dent's tense stance. "I've never killed *anyone*. I've never even been in a serious altercation."

That could change any second, Dent wanted to say. Instead, he went with, "Amy was. In my town ... and yours. I think our records say more about the different kind of men we are than the towns we watch over."

Dillard's face tightened like leather drying in the sun. Dent held his own expression still, but the remark had hit home and he was glad. In his estimation, he'd laid a painful but accurate truth on his fellow law enforcement officer.

Dillard, however, found a way to twist it. "Exactly. I believe there are other ways to handle criminals besides shooting them or hanging them."

"Gentlemen." Amy slapped her hands on the table as if to keep them from flying up and slapping one of them. "I insist we keep this friendly or you can both leave and I'll have the chicken and the library to myself."

Dent and Dillard squared off with hard looks, but after a moment, Dillard acquiesced with a shrug. "Amy's right, Sheriff. My apologies. I guess I'm just not used to *Western* law enforcement tactics. Violence and brute force over civility."

Dent was inclined to give Dillard a close-up introduction to the tactics, but a tussle would have to wait for another time. In the name of civility, he tamped down the desire to throw a punch at those perfect teeth. "Yes, she's right. Let's just have a pleasant meal and forget all about our differences."

With curt nods, both men agreed to bury the hatchet for the next half hour.

The meal continued, and out of respect for Amy, the tension settled to a low boil. Dent suspected at some point he and Dillard would have to settle things the *Western* way—with violence, brute force, and all. He looked forward to it.

Dillard didn't say anything else on the matter. In fact, he didn't have anything else to say to Dent at all. Finished with his third piece of chicken, he wiped off his hands and ambled over to his coat. "I believe I'll head on back to my room. We've done enough here today, don't you think, Amy?"

"Certainly. I'll see you tomorrow after school."

"I'll be here." He smiled, a charming expression for her, but it melted away instantly when his eyes met Dent's. "Sheriff, please give the doctor's wife my thanks for the food."

Dent nodded, a quick, curt movement.

When the outer door closed, Amy let out a long, heavy breath and hit him with soulful, pleading eyes. "Does it have to be that hard every time you two are around each other?"

"If you'll recall the conversation, I didn't start it off badly. He did."

She strolled over to him and laid her hands on his chest. She didn't speak, but her sultry expression invited him and he hooked his hands behind her back. "No, you didn't start it. He was rude. I just wish you two could be friends."

"I suppose anything is possible."

She chuckled and held his gaze. Every time he caught his reflection in her spectacles, he wanted to ... well, marry her for one thing. The open window behind him allowed in a breeze that stirred the delicate wisps of hair around her face. Then the soft strumming of a neighbor's lilting guitar reached his ears.

Amy heard it, too. "What a shame you don't dance." She slid her arms around his neck. "That song is called *Darcy Farrow's Lament* and it is a simple melody. I love to dance and I would love to dance with you. Why don't you let me teach you?"

He warred with pulling her closer or letting her go as an

answer. Before he could choose, she tightened her grip. He wasn't going anywhere. "I just don't dance," he whispered, brushing his lips over hers. "Isn't that good enough?"

Pouting, she pulled back. "I don't understand you. Most men find holding a young lady in their arms and twirling to the strains of a romantic ballad ... enticing. Am I not enticing?" She peered seductively at him over her spectacles.

Enticing? Just the thought of how enticing she was made sweat pop out on Dent's lip. He swiped a hand across his mouth. "I made a fool of myself once in front of the whole town. There's plenty of folks here who would remember it. I don't care to repeat the disaster, is all."

"What happened?"

"I was fourteen and Bonnie Stiles tried to teach me to dance at her sister's wedding." The memory still made him want to turn tail and run. Bonnie had never lived it down, which is why she now resided in Denver. "I was horsin' around instead of trying to be serious. I got us all tangled up and we hit the floor ... and Bonnie's skirt flew over her head and showed everybody at the wedding her bloomers."

Amy laughed, but bit it off like a door closing when Dent scowled at her.

"Yeah, I know it sounds funny but she never got over the humiliation. Every boy in town called her Bonnie Bloomers till she left Evergreen."

Amy pondered the strange story. After a moment, she reached up and touched Dent's face. Her hand was warm and felt like silk. "Sometimes, I would argue, you are blinded by pride." She paused, he assumed, to let that sink in, then sighed. "It hurts a little that you won't give me the gift of a dance."

"But I'd give you my life." It came out sounding so much more serious than he had intended. But he meant it. "Truly.

I'd take a bullet for you and not think twice about it. That doesn't mean anything?"

Perhaps not the most romantic thing he could say to a woman, but her stance softened nonetheless. Once again she wrapped her arms around his neck. "You know, Dent, it's possible for a man and a woman to give their lives to each other and no one need die in the process."

CHAPTER 6

Amy pulled her brush through her hair and studied her reflection in the vanity mirror. Her hair shimmered like strands of molasses in the low lamplight. Dent liked her hair. Loved her. She smiled as her mind drifted back to her conversation with him. She would take a bullet for him, too. But then her forehead creased. Amy couldn't fathom what made the bond between them so strong, so real.

She had no doubt he *would* take a bullet for her if the circumstance arose. Sometimes, though, things needn't be so deadly. Sometimes, a woman just wanted to step into her man's arms, look into his eyes, and twirl about the dance floor. No gunplay necessary to prove affection.

The joke slowed the brush in her hand, then it stopped. He'd hung eighteen men. Killed twenty-two.

Men like that don't just wash off the stink of death.

Yes. Yes, they do. Don't they, Lord? Dent wasn't so hardened by his life as a manhunter that he couldn't love—couldn't be selfless and giving?

Couldn't give her one dance?

A knock on her door snapped her out of the gloomy

musings. "Just a moment!" She snatched her robe off the foot of her bed and hurried to the front door, sure Dent had decided to come back for one more goodnight kiss. Only, she was once more disappointed. "Jeremy? What are you doing here? I was about to go to bed."

He twirled his derby in his hands with short, crisp movements, like a man with troubled thoughts. "I—I ..." He shrugged. "I just wanted to say goodnight."

Amy leaned on the door, sad for him. "Jeremy, I'm sorry. Are you sure you should be here? I mean in Evergreen."

He sighed and gazed up at the roof. "I just wanted a cup of coffee." He came back to her and winked, trying to be charming. "You can leave the door open."

That wicked grin of his always loosened her resolve. "Very well. Yes. Fine." She stepped back. "But you're right, the door does stay open. Better yet, stay on the porch and I'll bring the coffee out."

She and Jeremy sat in silence for a spell, enjoying the rhythm of rocking chairs, the fresh coffee and peaceful song of crickets. Within a few minutes the moon rose, washing her yard in silver shadows.

"This is nice," he said softly.

"Mmm-hmmm." But she wished for another to be beside her.

He drummed his fingers on the rim of his cup, as if he was searching for something to say. "He's the interim sheriff. When is the election?"

"September. He'll win. He's been a fine sheriff so far."

"You don't think he'll get bored staying in this one little town? No outlaws to chase down? No hangings to officiate? Evergreen strikes me as pretty tame for someone like him."

"I suppose it would suit *you* better?" She had to admit, Dent had a made a good point regarding their policing records. He was a man of action and courage, if somewhat brash. Jeremy was amiable and loathe to act in violence. Evergreen did fit him better than—

Would Dent get bored? The thought hadn't occurred to her until Jeremy had brought it up. But Dent hadn't come to the decision to stay in Evergreen lightly. He knew what he was walking away from. He had made the choice to pursue a more peaceful life here.

"Amy," Jeremy leaned toward her. "I know this kind of man. He's a warrior, not a husband. A soldier, not a father. He'll need something to do and Evergreen won't give him the chance. He'll chafe at the bit."

"You don't know that." Her temper sparked. Jeremy didn't know anything about the past Dent had let go of ... even the decision to quit looking for the man who had killed his father. "He wants a life of peace now. He wants to start a family. You don't know him well enough to say such things about him."

"Maybe." Jeremy absently rolled the mug between his hands. "I think I do. And I just wanted you to know ... I'll be here."

At first she thought he meant emotionally. But his gaze said something else. "You mean *here* in Evergreen?"

He nodded.

"You're not going back to Ohio?"

"Not right away. I want to buy a place here first. See about a job or buying a business."

"Why?"

"I want you to know my intentions are pure, sincere, and passionate."

Amy pulled back from him. "You're wasting your time. I've tried to make you believe that, Jeremy. I don't want to lead you on."

"You're not. But I believe you will see Dent's true colors sooner rather than later. I want to be here for that."

"You care that much about me?"

"I thought I was abundantly clear on the issue."

"You *love* me?"

"Deeply and with all my heart."

Amy discovered to her surprise she was flattered and annoyed at the same time. Flattered by the attention, annoyed that Jeremy seemed intent on watching Dent fail. He was so sure. She found his confidence unnerving.

Dent loves me. He would die for me. "Would you take a bullet for me, Jeremy?"

His eyes widened at the question. "I—I ... Well, yes, of course."

Amy wasn't sure why the question had leaped out of her mouth, but Jeremy's answer—the surprise, the hesitation—sealed his fate as the runner-up. No greater love ... "Good night, Jeremy."

"You look like a man who could use a friend."

In the noisy restaurant, Dent had somehow managed to close out the world and was surprised by the *hello*. He smiled up at Audra Drysdale—er, Pine now, he reminded himself again. "Howdy, Audra." He motioned to his plate. "You and Dillon like to join me for some breakfast?"

"Don't mind if we do." She slid into the seat opposite him. "I'll go ahead and order for him. He'll be here soon as he's finished at the feedstore."

She was a pretty gal. A delicate, flawless face, nice curves, and loose waves of spun gold hair had every man in town slack-jawed and stupid. Except Dent. Somehow he'd always known she wasn't the one for him. "How is married life?"

"Well, when it feels like we're married, I'll let you know.

Right now, we're still courting." Her green eyes flashed with amusement and fire.

He almost asked how long she was going to put Dillon through this, but checked himself. What happened in the Pines' bedroom was certainly none of his business. She was enjoying dragging out Dillon's pain, though.

"How goes it with you and the schoolteacher?"

"All right, I reckon." Like he was about to talk to a woman about it.

"I heard you might have a little competition."

He stabbed his waffle. "No, I don't think so."

Audra rested her chin in the palm of her hand and batted innocent eyes at him. "You sure?"

"I'm sure." As he sawed his waffle into several pieces, a thought on a related note did occur to him. "Maybe you could help me with one thing, though, if you were of a mind to."

She straightened up, apparently tickled at the prospect of giving Dent some advice. "I am, absolutely."

"If I wanted to ask Amy to marry me ..." he drizzled maple syrup over his breakfast, dragging out the moment.

Audra leaned in. "Yes ..."

"How do I," he capped the syrup. "I mean, what could I do ...?" He shook his head in disgust. No way around this but to say it. "How do I make it special? Really ... magical? Not just a nice restaurant or a walk in the moonlight." He leaned toward her. "I want to make her speechless."

Audra grinned—big, wide, and beautiful. "You let me ask her some questions."

CHAPTER 7

A smiling, perky Audra Pine met Amy coming out of the schoolhouse. "Good afternoon, Amy."

"Audra. What a nice surprise."

"I hope so. I was wondering if you would like to join me for an ice cream. We don't get to talk much at church and I was thinking we should get to know each other better. It gets kinda lonely out at the ranch, just men everywhere."

Amy wasn't surprised by the invitation. She and Audra did see each other at church, but too often had an antsy man in tow. They had promised each other more than once to get together for a little shopping or a ride. Maybe Audra had resolved to make the extra effort at a friendship. Amy locked the schoolhouse door and smiled. "We've been meaning to sit with you at church, but Dent and I keep coming in late."

"Then let's take a few minutes to chat now."

"Unfortunately, I can't, Audra. You've heard about the books that Jeremy brought? I'm helping him set up the library."

"You can't spare fifteen minutes?"

Amy had to admit she loved vanilla ice cream. And could a woman have too many friends in a town the size of Evergreen?

What better way to find out than over something sweet? "Well, as long as you don't hold it against me for not being able to dawdle."

"Why, that's just fine. I don't have a lot of time myself, which is why I suggested ice cream."

Audra hooked her arm through Amy's and the two ambled toward town. "So, speaking of the library, I hear this Jeremy has intentions toward you. That can't be going over well with Dent."

"Oh, I think it bothers him some, yes, but I've put Jeremy in his place. Dent told me he'd take a bullet for me." Amy chuckled. "Not the most romantic thing, I suppose, but when I asked Jeremy if he'd do the same, he hesitated."

Silence said both women knew what that meant.

"Dent is romantic in his own unique way, it sounds like."

Again, Amy chuckled. "Yes. I suppose when he gets around to asking me to marry him, he'll just propose to me in the school or on my front porch." She sighed. "A safe, conventional proposal. I should be all right with that. I love him and he loves me."

"Do you ever have any doubts?"

Amy shook her head. "No. I have my moments when—" she shrugged, "well, I guess I wish he was a bit more romantic in the poetic sense. In the foolish sense. He can be very serious. And he's so hard on himself. That's why he won't dance."

"What? Why?"

"He made a fool of himself on the dance floor when he was younger and embarrassed the young lady he was dancing with. I think he's afraid he'll do the same to me."

Audra's brow creased and she bit her bottom lip. "That's so silly. I'm sure he could take a few lessons and be fine."

"I offered. It's almost ..." Amy hated to admit the truth, but she couldn't find a way around it. "Well, honestly, it hurts my feelings a little that he won't do something as simple as dance with me."

"Must not be so simple to him."

"Clearly."

"Does he show concern about other things that are important to you?"

"Yes. He's kind and gentle, and surprisingly sensitive for a man who's seen and done the things he's done. This is the first issue we've even come close to bumping heads over."

Both girls exchanged nods and pleasantries with a group of folks passing by, parents of some of Amy's students. A moment later, Amy could see the sign ahead advertising cold, hand-turned ice cream. "What about you and Dillon? Are you getting along well? Not that it's any of my business. Forgive me for being nosy."

Audra waved off the apology. "Not at all. I'm glad for the chance to talk about it. I can't figure him out. He's a perfect gentleman. Notice I emphasize the word *perfect*."

"Um, and you ...?" Amy felt a bit uncomfortable with the conversation. Did she really want to know if Audra and Dillon were intimate? "I take it, you would prefer less of a gentleman?"

"We are married, but he's taking things at a snail's pace. He says he loves me. I said I love him. We're married. I'm not sure what's standing in the way of ... intimacy."

"I couldn't begin to guess." And wouldn't try.

"I figure he either is waiting on me, or he's trying to figure out if he wants to stay. You heard about that, right?"

"That you agreed to let him go after a year?"

Blushing, Audra nodded. "The details aren't common

knowledge, but the whole town knows he and I are an arranged marriage. And I know that's been hard on him."

Amy flinched. "I can only imagine." She pondered Audra's predicament for a few more steps, and then said, "Maybe ... maybe he's trying to prove himself. To you and to the town."

"I hadn't thought of that."

"Men. And they say we're the mystery."

Laughing, the ladies stepped into the ice cream parlor.

"That's all you need us to do?" Susan blinked at Dent, her wood spoon paused in a steaming sauce pan. "Throw a party?"

"If you wouldn't mind." Dent grinned. "Next Friday night."

"Who would you like us to invite?"

"The whole dang town."

Susan cast a suspicious glance at Doc, standing in the kitchen doorway. The old man rubbed his bearded jaw and studied Dent. "You're going to ask her at the party, aren't you? Get down on one knee in front of a crowd. That takes courage. I'm proud of you, son."

Dent opted to neither confirm nor deny that guess. Asking Amy in such a traditional manner had its merits, he supposed. And it might come to that if he lost his nerve. His plan, however, was his secret.

Both men looked at Susan, knowing full well she would have an opinion as well. She laid the spoon down on the stove. "I don't know, Dent. You sure she wouldn't prefer something more private? More intimate? Like a buggy ride in the moonlight?"

"I'm not sure of anything anymore." He certainly would have preferred this not get so complicated, but he'd come to the conclusion love was not ever going to be simple. He twirled his hat in his hands. "I wish I could just take her for a buggy ride and ask her without an audience, but I don't think that—I mean, I think have something ... to prove to her."

"What's that?" Doc asked. "What have you got to prove?"

Dent thought about it for a moment. "Well, you'd think it would be enough that I would take a bullet for her. Pastor told me even Jesus Himself said there was no greater love than for a man to lay down his life for another person." He shook his head, mystified by the way a woman's mind worked. "But for offering marriage, that just doesn't seem to be enough."

Susan leaned forward, her eyes shining with excitement. "Why? What do you have planned?"

"Thank you for your help." Dent dropped his hat back in place. "I'm heading out. Got some place to be."

"Amy and the library?" Doc asked.

Dent didn't want to lie. "Not tonight. I've got some business to attend to."

"I wouldn't leave her alone with that fella too much," the old physician warned.

"You think he could steal her in a week?" Dent was only half-kidding. Was this a harebrained idea and should he be more worried about tending to Amy than this proposal?

"No," Susan said firmly, bending down to check something in the oven. "Not in a week. Not in a lifetime."

---

*A*my checked her mail once a week on Fridays. It seemed a lighthearted thing to do to usher in the weekend, and if she had anything, she could make time Saturday morning to answer. The letter the postmaster handed her piqued her curiosity.

She thanked him and wandered outside, the boardwalk squeaking beneath her feet. She caught a whiff of sage and pine blowing in from the prairie as she stared at the handwriting. Rough, scrawled, in dark pencil. Not a refined hand, either. A man's hand, so familiar ... The return address was simply Care of Prairie Church, Rifle, Colorado.

"Who do I know in Rifle, Colorado, for goodness sake?" Curiosity getting the better of her, Amy hurried over to the post office's bench and sat. Readjusting her glasses, she tore open the envelope and pulled out the letter. After only a few sentences, tears filled her eyes and her heart pounded in her chest as she read.

Israel.

Dear Miss Tate, first, if you were worried, please do not be. I am fine. I hope you are fine, too. Maybe I should not have writ to you, but you were so kind to me, both when I was your pupil and when I was in jail with Pa.

There were several places in the letter where Israel had scratched through words and tried again. He seemed to have made a concentrated effort to spell as many words right as possible.

I was afraid you might be worrying over me, so I have risked this note.

I am a working cowboy at a ranch. I have been in no trouble and do not plan on getting into any. Someday I hope to ride back through Evergreen and see you, but that may never happen. I do not know. I am a wanted man there.

If you would like to write back, please address your letter to the Prairie Church. The pastor here is helping me with my schooling, and he will get me your letter. I read real good now but my spelling needs much help.

God bless you.
Sincerely,
Israel

Crying with joy, Amy pressed the letter to her heart. *Oh, God, how wonderful. He's all right. Thank You, thank You—*

Her joy mixed with fear. Could she tell Dent? Should she? He'd let the boy go once. Was it fair to ask him to keep this secret from the long arm of the law?

Until she could decide, it would be her secret alone.

CHAPTER 8

Dent stared at the new wanted poster, some fella named Cherokee Bob, but his mind wouldn't stop going back to Amy. He laid the poster on his desk and leaned back in his chair. He sure didn't miss his life of anger and vengeance, of cold meals, cold nights, and hard beds. Turned out, this soft life of policing a small town was all right. Six months ago he would have never believed he'd be doing this —and be so happy about it.

Amy. She'd had a powerful impact on his whole way of thinking. For years he'd ridden out as a U.S. marshal intent on finding his father's killers. Over and over he'd hunted down, arrested, even hung criminals—every one a substitute for the murderer. The thirst for revenge had consumed Dent's every breath, every heartbeat, every bullet he'd fired. Then he'd met a pretty little schoolmarm who'd convinced him there was more to live for than hate.

There was love.

Because of Amy, he'd even done the unspeakable for a lawman: he'd willingly let a prisoner escape. A sixteen-year-old boy guilty only of having a lousy father.

No, that's not fair.

Disgusted, Dent pushed back from his desk and swiveled to the window overlooking Evergreen's Main Street, flowing at a relaxed pace with nice, peaceable folks. Amy had softened him some for sure, in a good way. Letting Israel escape —that was all on him. He'd wanted the kid to have a chance because with a father ready to testify against him to save his own skin, there was no chance. Dent couldn't see that one arrest through. All Amy had done was get him to accept that the law wasn't always in the right, especially if the spirit of it was being used to twist justice.

And somehow all this had brought him 'round to considering God. That a man needed a higher source of wisdom than his own—since his own could be faulty and riddled with inconsistencies.

The door jangled and Dent looked up and had to hold back a sigh. Yet another opportunity to chat with Dillard. The man pulled off his derby and smiled, but it was a wolf's snarl in disguise. "Sheriff, do you have a moment?"

Nothing he'd rather say than *no*, but curiosity got the better of him. "Have a seat."

"I got the invitation to your little party." Dillard settled in the chair across from him and crossed a foot over his knee. "I've tried the patient tactic. I think now I should quit wasting time."

"So do I." Dent picked up a pencil and started walking it through his fingers, waiting.

"I understand for years you looked for your father's murderer." Dillard set his hat on the desk. "Under the guise of your U.S. Marshal badge."

Dent didn't respond. Just kept walking the pencil.

Dillard lifted his chin, apparently accepting the silence as a sign to continue. "Clues did lead you to a name. Tom Newcomb, an alias for Joe Hayes, a person whom the previous sheriff in this town may have been aware of but—strangely—didn't pursue."

The slight smear of Ben's name didn't sit well with Dent. Ben had had his reasons for stopping the investigation. His own son had killed Dent's father. The man was still at large, but the trail had grown cold and Dent had lost heart. "I thought you said you were going to quit wasting time?"

Dillard's lips narrowed at the jab. "Fine. I know who killed your father. I know where he is. I know that you can bring him back to Cheyenne to face justice. You just have to make one little trade."

Dent needed a moment to absorb the statements, check the wound that Dillard ripped open. Dent had had almost this exact conversation with Mayor Coker—the man who had shot Amy. Why—*how*—did these men keep getting this information? It riled him no small amount that peoples' lives were just pawns to some people. Even more, he was sick and tired of them dangling his pa's killer in front of him like a carrot on a stick.

Dent lashed down the desire to beat Jeremy Dillard to within an inch of his life, but the storm brewing in his soul scared him. He wasn't sure he could hold his seething anger toward him in anymore. Teeth clenched, he leaned forward. "I know who killed my father. Joe, Ben's son. Coker told me."

"But Coker didn't know where to find him. I do."

He knew? Jeremy Dillard, of all people, knew where Joe Hayes was hiding? Fury warred within him. Why now? Why did this have to come up now when he was so ready to walk away from the past and look ahead with Amy?

Dillard could be lying. But what if he really knew Joe's whereabouts? Did Dent want to know? "I don't believe you, Dillard. I think you're just trying to make trouble for Amy and me. You think I'll ride out after the man, don't you?"

Dillard lifted an eyebrow. "Honestly, yes, we do."

"We?"

"Amy's father hired me to ... disrupt this wedding. It was more fun the other way, flirting with her and all, but she's quite enamored of you. Solid as a rock. Loyal as the day is long. I'd say you're a lucky man, only I know you're about to let it all go."

Dent deflated and fell back into his chair. Amy's father ...? Before he could ask the question, Dillard answered. "Because you're no good for his daughter. He and I both were hoping I could come out here and sweep her off her feet, but, as I said, I don't think that's doable. At least not right now. Mr. Tate is a smart man, however. He went ahead and put enough Pinkertons on this case to find your father's killer. You getting the name from Coker was tremendously helpful."

Dent's mind reeled from all the revelations. He wouldn't deny the disappointment, either. He'd never even met Amy's father, but the man had decided Dent wasn't good enough for her? He pinched the bridge of his nose and gathered his thoughts. Forcing himself to put aside the personal insult, he snapped his gaze back to Dillard. "Where's Joe?"

"I said there was a trade."

The fury in Dent went from a low boil to an erupting volcano in an instant. He leaped from his chair, grabbed Dillard by the throat and pressed him into the back rest. "How about your freedom for the trade? How about I don't put you under arrest for interfering in an investigation?"

Dillard took a swipe at Dent, catching him in the jaw. Dent's head snapped back as pain rattled his brain. He released Dillard's throat and jabbed the man hard in the nose. Dillard shook it off and lunged for Dent. The two scuffled, entwined, trading short, painful punches.

Hate and fear burned in Dillard's dark eyes. "She's too good for you," he snarled, throwing a punch.

Dent dodged it, but the fire left him. He didn't want to

fight. He just wanted peace. An end to this chapter of his life. He needed Joe's location.

"Let it go, Dillard," he growled. "Tell me where Joe is." Dent blocked a punch, swung in response, delivering a hammer blow to Dillard's jaw. The man's eyes rolled into the back of his head and he melted to the floor like a wax doll hit with a furnace blast.

CHAPTER 9

"Dent, I'm asking this time. Am I interrupting?"
Dent appreciated the pastor's respect, and shook his head.

The reverend settled on the same pew with him, but Dent didn't look over. He was drawn again to that cross on the wall. Christ had died on that thing. He'd had a mission. A duty to perform. He had prayed for a different outcome, but had followed through when the time came.

His mission had saved humanity. Who would Dent save if he went through with his? Love and duty. The line between the two—once so sharp and clear—had grown blurry.

"I'm looking forward to the party tonight. Susan said it may be a very important evening for you and Amy."

Dent flinched and dropped his gaze to his hands. He wasn't sure if the night was going to turn out like he'd hoped.

Pastor nodded, moving past the small talk. "Trouble in Paradise?"

"I've got that Dillard fella locked up. He threw a punch at me." Not a lie, but Dent had been the one to start the brawl.

"Oh, my." He scratched his chin. "That's going to come as quite a surprise to Amy. I understand they're friends."

"Yes, sir." Dent worked his jaw back and forth, wondering just why he was here. To learn from Christ's sacrifice, his obedience? But did duty trump everything? Where did Dent's first duty lie? With the law or Amy? When did love win? He thought he knew the answer, knew what he had to do. He hoped Pastor Wills could talk him out of it.

"But there's something else?"

Dent nodded. "Dillard said he was hired by Amy's father to come stop our engagement."

Pastor Wills's eyebrows rose almost to his receding hairline.

"When that didn't look like it was going to work, he told me something. Amy's father hired some detectives. They found my father's killer. Joe, Ben's son."

Pastor Wills dragged in a long, weary breath. "The man you hunted for—what, eight years?"

"He knows I'll go after him. Amy's father, I mean. Dillard, too." Dent looked at Pastor. "I have to. Don't I?"

"I think only you can answer that, Dent."

"I love Amy. More than my own life. I never thought I'd ever find Joe. I had given up. I was willing to let it all go, but I'm a lawman ..."

"And you have your duty?"

"Yes."

"Duty is not obsession. It's not vengeance. Are you clear on that now?"

Dent would never let hate, never let the unquenchable thirst for revenge master his life again. The truth had set him free. He wore a badge. He would honor it. *And* his fathers: the memory of the earthly one, the love of the heavenly One. "Yes."

ASK ME TO MARRY YOU

"Then I think Amy will understand you have to go after this man."

"And let her go." he said, looking up at heaven. Amy had been a shelter for Dent. A place of rest and peace. The thought of wrecking that—*her*—again made his heart writhe in pain. "I don't want to bring this tornado—my past—down on her. And what do I tell her about her father?"

"One thing I've learned in all my years following Christ, you can always trust love." He rested a hand on Dent's shoulder. "If not anyone else's, you can trust His. He will never leave you or forsake you. And He'll help you with these decisions."

Dent's gaze drifted back to the cross. "Why does love always have to be about sacrifice?"

"Because if it's not, it isn't love."

Amy could have sworn she was walking on air as she hurried home to her little cabin. The sky overhead was a cloudless, stunning sapphire. The spring breeze refreshed her soul, and her heart soared with the sparrows. Israel was alive and doing well.

She couldn't think of anything that could make her happier, except perhaps—

"Amy."

Dent.

Whirling around, she saw him coming out of the church. He'd been talking to Pastor Wills? Could that be a sign of future plans? He jogged across the street to her, dark hair dancing beneath his hat, brown eyes flashing. They laced their fingers together and Amy read the longing in his tender expression, but they didn't kiss on the street.

"On your way home?"

"I am, Sheriff."

"May I walk with you?"

She nodded, delighted with his company, but a flicker of something gloomy in his expression lowered her spirits. Then she remembered that she couldn't share with him the good news about Israel—at least not yet—and that weighed even more on her heart.

Arm-in-arm they strolled down the street, the traffic here at the edge of town sparse. A flock of chickens wandered around the livery stable, pecking at the ground with great deliberation.

Dent and Amy remained quiet until they reached the outskirts. "You were coming from the church," she finally said. "I'm a little surprised by that. Can I ask why you were there, or is it private?"

Dent sniffed and shook his head. "No, I want to tell you. Some of it's just not easy to put into words."

She nodded, waiting, willing to let him find his way.

"You're gonna hear soon enough. I have Dillard in jail."

She leaped back from him. "What?"

"He started a little bit of a scuffle with me."

Amy couldn't comprehend. She blinked and took another step back. The pain in Dent's eyes, though, brought her back to him. Searching his face, she rested her hands on his shoulders. "What happened?"

Dent dropped his hands to her waist. "This isn't easy to say."

She nodded. "Just say it."

"Your father sent Dillard here to break us up. When that didn't work, he dangled a carrot."

Amy frowned. That her father would stoop to something as manipulative as interfering in her love life didn't surprise her. She was deeply disappointed he hadn't given Dent a chance. But what of this carrot? "My father has a tendency to overstep his bounds, Dent. I'm sorry. What's he done now?"

"He found my father's killer."

A sense of dread cascaded over Amy. Mayor Coker had dangled a similar form of this bait, revealing the killer's name, and tearing out Dent's heart in the process. Now he would go through all that agony again? She touched his cheek. "Where is he?"

"It doesn't matter. I'm not going after him."

At first, joy surged through her. He had said he was done with the darkness—the addiction to revenge, the constant dance with death. He had left it all behind. But something didn't feel right. "Dent, I know you're still dealing with guilt over letting Israel go. Are you sure you want to let this go, too?"

He took too long to answer. "Yes. I thought long and hard about it. You might even say I prayed. At first I wanted to leave today, but I sat still and tried to listen. I—I—" he seemed to flounder for words— "I just want to build a life with you, Amy. I've decided you're more important to me than anything. Including this."

She sighed and looked down at the ground. "You're a good lawman now, Dent. I mean, you wear the badge for justice, not vengeance. Right?" She came back to him. "Right?"

"Yes." He tilted his head, his brow creasing with suspicion. "But that doesn't mean—"

"If I said you should go and arrest this man, with my blessing, would you? Would my opinion matter?"

"No. Maybe. I don't know. What are you saying?"

"That I don't want this left hanging out there for the rest of our lives. If you believe you can find and arrest this man, I think it would be good for you."

Dent pulled his hands away from her and stepped back. Confusion, sadness, played out on his face.

She clutched his vest and pulled him back to her. "I love you, Dent. And I know you'll always wonder. I think if you close this chapter, you'll be whole. I think you can do this for the right reason now. Justice."

He caressed her cheek. "Aren't you afraid I'll ... get lost?"

"Not in the old darkness. I'm terrified you'll get hurt or worse. But I'm more afraid your heart won't heal completely if you don't do this. You're not the same man you were. You are better. So, I'm willing to let you prove it to yourself."

"Your sacrifice," he whispered so softly she almost missed it.

"What?"

"Nothing." He leaned down and kissed her, bringing the spark of joy back to their conversation. "Why don't we just focus on the party tonight. I'm gonna have the prettiest gal in Wyoming on my arm. I am one lucky man."

Amy was a bit surprised when Doc showed up at her door instead of Dent. For a moment, she wondered if her sheriff had headed out after his father's killer. She opened the door to greet the physician, and the old man stopped, halfway up her porch steps.

"My gracious." He let out a long whistle of appreciation. "If you aren't going to be the belle of the ball."

Amy patted the powder blue velvet skirt. "My mother sent a few of my things." She touched the diamond choker at her neck. "Including my jewelry. It's not too much, is it?"

"No, ma'am," he said firmly. "You look like you stepped right out of the window at the House of Worth. I bet you'll

ASK ME TO MARRY YOU

strike Dent dumb at the sight of you. I'd put money on it. Better yet, I'd pay to see it."

Amy giggled over the compliments and fluffed her skirt, wondering if the bustle was a bit too much for a small party. "It's rather formal, but I haven't dressed up in so long."

"Perfect," he said with as much spunk as before. "It's perfect." He offered his arm. "Let's go wow the town."

"Speaking of the town, is that what's held Dent up? I thought he was escorting me." She had toyed with the idea of telling him about Israel on the way to the party, but had decided against it.

"Oh, he'll be there. Just running a little late."

Glowing Chinese lanterns filled Doc and Susan's backyard, along with half the town. There was barely room to move, given the crowd and the picnic tables covered in food. Amy was taken aback by the number of guests.

"What's the occasion?" she asked Doc as he led her through the packed bodies. "I didn't realize this was going to be such a big gathering." She nodded and smiled at several people as he pulled her over to Susan.

Standing at the head of a table covered in delicious treats, the woman gasped and clasped her hands together. "Amy, that dress is simply stunning. Poor Dent's liable to faint dead away when he sees you."

"Kinda what I was thinking," Doc said as he shook a neighbor's hand in passing. Through the murmuring of the crowd Amy heard a violin tuning up. A flute joined it, followed by a cello. "Susan said we're going to have *chamber music* tonight." Doc scanned the crowd, scowling. "I'd prefer some polkas."

"Oh, you," Susan swatted at him. "Why don't you go get us some punch?"

"All righty." Doc nodded and headed off into the laughing, chatting mass of bodies.

"It's a lovely party, Susan." Amy glanced around, taking in the crowd, filled now with many, many faces she knew—unlike the fall festival last year when she had been new to the town and unsure of everything. "Far bigger than you led me to believe. Is there an occasion? Should I have brought a gift?"

"No, no. We, uh, just wanted to celebrate spring."

The band struck up something classical. Amy guessed it might be Strauss's *Blue Danube*. "I didn't know anyone in Evergreen could play classical music."

Susan laughed. "No one can. These fellas came over from Cheyenne."

"My, you're really putting on the dog tonight."

A sly little smile tipped Susan's lips. "I hope you enjoy it." Suddenly, the woman's gaze shot past Amy and her eyes widened to the size of harvest moons. "My, oh, my. Dent?"

Amy spun. And her breath caught in her chest. Her handsome sheriff, dressed so often in simple trousers, a cotton shirt, and a worn vest, had traded all that for an elegant, perfectly tailored tuxedo. It accentuated his broad shoulders and narrow waist to perfection. His boots glistened with fresh polish, a red rose hung on his lapel. The stark, white shirt seemed to glow. His tanned, clean-shaven face made her want to kiss every inch of it.

He was magnificent.

And Jeremy thought he could compete with my sheriff?

Dent's dark eyes danced with mirth and warmth. His gaze strolled leisurely over her gown, and she saw the spark of desire ignite. He approached her and Amy realized she was holding her breath.

"Amy ..." He shook his head. "I don't have the words." He swallowed. "You are beautiful. The most stunning thing I've ever seen."

She exhaled and smiled. "Thank you, Sheriff. When you didn't come for me, I thought maybe you'd already left to get Joe."

"Joe's not going anywhere. U.S. marshals arrested him in Colorado today. Judge Lynch has already signed the extradition order. I'll go get him in a few days." Amy tilted her head and studied Dent. He tugged on his collar and scanned his tuxedo. "What? Something wrong with this suit?"

Yes, indeed, he was so handsome he made her heart race. But it wasn't his looks causing this reaction in her. He exuded confidence. And peace. Like a man who had conquered a huge challenge. She was delirious; beside herself with happiness for him. He could finally let his father rest. "I was just thinking how lucky I am."

He plucked her hand from her side. "Turned out to be a nice, well-attended party, huh?"

A little surprised by the abrupt change in subject, she slipped her arm around his waist to hold him close and revel in him. "Yes, it is."

"Everybody in town seems to be here."

"It appears so," she agreed, wondering why this sudden fascination with the size of the party.

"Wonder where they got that high-toned musical group from." Something in his voice sounded amused.

"Susan said Cheyenne." She peered up at him, deciding the turn in conversation was a man's way of moving past the sensitive, hearts-and-flowers kind of talk.

Dent turned and looked over the crowd again, his head cocked as if he was listening to the song. "You're too pretty not to be out there dancing."

Amy fought the urge to try once more to convince him to dance. "I'm fine right where I am."

Dent shook his head and cut his eyes sideways at her. "Nah, you should be twirling and spinning, showing off that gown." He offered her his hand. "Miss Tate, would you do me the honor of dancing with me?"

Amy's mouth went slack. "Do you mean it?"

"I didn't do all this," he motioned to the party around them, "just to watch you dance with some other fella."

"You did ... all this?" Amy couldn't fathom. Why? What was—?

Dent slipped his arm around her and pulled her in close. "Offering to take a bullet for you didn't seem to impress you." He cupped her chin. "I want to marry you. I want to spend the rest of my life with you. And if the price for that is that I have to dance with you ... Amy Tate, it'll be my privilege, my *honor* to do so. I'm only sorry I made you unhappy over something so small."

Amy fought the knot in her throat, but her tears wouldn't be stopped. "It wasn't small to you."

"Yes, it was. Compared to how happy it could have made you, it was small and I was selfish. Love is sacrifice. I make this one willingly."

He led her to the front of the crowd where a small space was open. To her amazement, with great skill and confidence, Dent put an arm around her and proceeded to lead her in a perfect waltz. "I thought you said you couldn't dance."

"I learned."

"From whom?"

"Audra and Dillon. Doc and Susan. They gave me a few lessons."

A wry, half-smile played on his lips. He was quite pleased with himself. And so was Amy. "Dent, now *I* don't have the words to tell you how much this all means to me." He spun her, box-stepped, twirled her again. Amy couldn't get over his skill. "It's—it's grand. It's magical."

"So, you're happy. Is that what I'm hearing?"

"Delirious."

"This *is* better than me getting shot for you."

"Much."

"I guess there's just one more thing to do then."

"Which is?"

Dent stopped her, held her gaze with his dark, intense eyes, and slipped to one knee. Teasing her with slow, deliberate movements, he drew a ring from his pocket. "Amy, will you dance with me the rest of my life?"

Grinning, she cupped his cheeks and nodded. The crowd erupted in cheers, startling them both. But they both laughed as he slipped the ring on her finger. She pulled him to his feet and kissed him with joy and determination.

"I love you, Sheriff."

"I love you, Amy."

"Finish our dance?"

He didn't answer with words. Instead, he raised her hand and waltzed with her to a perfect, soaring rendition of *Blue Danube*.

Amy had never enjoyed a dance more.

"The circuit judge will be around next week. You can pay your fine or plead your case." Dent slid Dillard's hat and wallet across his desk to the man. "I'd suggest you pay the fine and head back to Swanton. This goes to trial, you'll lose and wind up sitting in my jail for assaulting an officer."

A slimy little grin twitched on Dillard's lips. He deposited the wallet in his breast pocket and picked up his little derby.

"Sheriff, I've decided I like Evergreen. I think I'm going to stay around."

"Amy mentioned you were thinking along those lines."

"Any objections?"

"Plenty." *I'd object less to a hoard of spiders infesting the town.* "But I'm the sheriff, not God. A man can live where he pleases in this country."

"And what if you weren't the sheriff? What would you do with yourself? Go back to the U.S. Marshals? Become a bounty hunter?"

The questions raised Dent's suspicions. "You going to run against me?"

Dillard's smile broke into a full grin. "The thought had occurred to me. I'd have a good shot at it. I have the experience, the financial backing thanks to Amy's father, and the political skill."

Dent had never run for anything in his life. With every breath, he disliked Dillard more and more. And until a few moments ago, he hadn't thought that possible. "If I lost to you, I'd still have Amy." He plucked his gun belt off the back of his chair and started strapping it on, while enjoying the cold, hard expression on Dillard's face. Dent had to hold back a chuckle. "I guess I'll see you around then." He grabbed his hat off the rack and headed out to do his patrols.

---

*I*f you enjoyed *Ask Me to Marry You*, **your review** would be so appreciated! I recognize that your time is a precious commodity, and I am truly grateful for the investment of it in my stories. Reviews posted anywhere help retailers make a decision whether to promote me or not, and your opinion also helps a fellow reader considering this story. Thank you again for sharing your thoughts!

And

Please subscribe to my newsletter
to receive updates on my new releases and other fun news.
You'll also receive a FREE e-book—
A Lady in Defiance, The Lost Chapters
just for subscribing!

SNEAK PEEK

Mail-Order Deception
(Brides of Evergreen Book 3)

Intrepid reporter Ellie Blair gets an undercover assignment as a mail-order bride and heads off to Wyoming where she discovers her potential groom isn't what he appears to be, either.

Boston — June, 1890

"Mr. Taylor would like to see you in his office."

Ellie Blair absently shrugged off the tap on her shoulder and continued writing her story. Harvey Wiggins, the World Daily News' fidgety, freckled-faced copyboy, cleared his throat nervously. "He said now, Miss Blair."

The twelve men sitting at the long conference table working on their own stories all stopped their chattering to listen. Their stares made her uncomfortable, but, as always, she hid it. "Fine. Thank you, Harvey."

The boy nodded and raced off. Ellie slowly laid her pencil down, wishing she could answer the summons without every other reporter at the table gawking.

"Got another scoop in the works, Nellie—er, I mean, Ellie?" Jack Conway asked. A veteran reporter, he'd made it abundantly clear from the day Ellie was hired women belonged in the kitchen. To add insult to injury, he purposely mixed up her name with that *other* female reporter. Oh, how Ellie hated Nellie Bly and her showy publicity stunts.

"I don't know, Jack," she said rising. "But don't worry. If it is, I'll hand you the first paper off the press."

A rumble of laughter circled the table.

"Maybe he's gonna make you head of the *Ladies Fashion* department." Bill Reese snickered and tugged at his loud, red-and-yellow plaid jacket. The reporter was famous not for his writing, but for his vulgar taste in suits. The other reporters joked he frightened small animals and children with those clothes.

Regardless, Ellie wasn't in the mood today to tolerate these men or their ridiculous insults. "Well, if he does, Bill," she walked past him slowly, "I'll have you moved over. Seeing as how the style section doesn't need good reporters—just hacks—you'll fit right in."

Laughter followed Ellie as she strode across the newsroom. Her smug satisfaction, though, quickly gave way to a twinge of guilt over her comments. *But, Lord, they never let up. I can't do anything right because I'm a woman. If they can sling insults, so can I.*

Conviction almost stopped her in her tracks. No, there was never a reason to sling insults. *Bless those who curse you, pray for those who spitefully use you.*

Clenching her teeth, she prayed for forgiveness and knocked on Mr. Taylor's glass door.

A handsome man in his early fifties, a little gray salting

his dark brown hair, he dropped the notepad he was holding and waved her in. "Ellie, have a seat." He half-rose from his own, motioning to the chair opposite him.

"Thank you. Harvey said you wanted to see me."

They both sat, Ellie on the edge of her seat to make room for her bustle. Mr. Taylor picked up the notepad, but didn't look at it. "I got a call today from the O'Toole Private Detective Agency. The owner, Michael O'Toole, would like to meet with you regarding an investigation."

That sounded promising. "Does he have a tip for me?"

Mr. Taylor jiggled the notepad. "I think he may. Listen," he dropped the pad again and leaned back in his chair, as if to get a better look at her. "That piece you did on corruption in the alderman's office was as sharp and clean as they come. You've got a real future in journalism, even if you are a female."

Ellie's eyebrow twitched at the backhanded compliment.

"So, I would give you two pieces of advice." He plucked a cigar from his breast pocket and sniffed it. "Trust is the most important thing a reporter can bring to an investigation." He pointed the smoke at her. "Build trust and a source will sing the National Anthem for you. But I think you've got that one down."

"And the second?"

He took his time rummaging his desk for a match, lighting his smoke, enjoying a long puff. Slowly, he exhaled, smoke swirling around his head. "I know you flirted a little to get that clerk in the alderman's office to open up to you." Heat rose to Ellie's cheeks and Mr. Taylor laughed. "Relax, kid, I'm not gonna bust your chops for that. My second little nugget is, use all the tools in your bag to get your story. Those are the reporters who make it in this business, the ones who pull out all the stops."

Good advice, of course, but Ellie had a second twinge of

SNEAK PEEK

guilt. Had manipulating a person, the way she had that clerk, really been the only way to get the story?

"That said, Ellie Blair, you be careful dealing with Michael O'Toole."

The warning redirected her thoughts to the matter at hand. "I was under the impression the O'Toole Agency is a respected investigation firm."

"The company is legitimate. Loaded with good detectives. It's O'Toole you gotta watch. Whatever he wants to see you about," he waved the cigar in the air, "be skeptical. Rely on your instincts, kid. You got good ones."

"He didn't say what this was about?"

"Only that he had something a good reporter would drool over."

"But why me? Why didn't he ask for Jack or Bill?"

"He said they just wouldn't do."

"So, you offered them? Because they're men?"

Mr. Taylor's mouth lifted in one corner and he took another casual puff. "I offered them because they have fifty years' experience combined. You've got two." Her indignation must have shown. He leaned forward and crushed the cigar in his ashtray. "He wants a woman with a spirit of adventure for this potential scoop of his. Now Jack and Bill are pretty adventurous, but I don't think I could pay either of them enough to slip into a skirt." Ellie pressed her fingers to her lips to hide the smile. Mr. Taylor chuckled. "You're one up there on my veteran reporters, Ellie. So, go see if O'Toole has a story you can sink your teeth into."

Why had this Michael O'Toole asked for her? Ellie wasn't the only female reporter in the city of Boston, though the pool was small.

She paused with her hand on the O'Toole Detective Agency's door. The excitement of the unexpected invitation wearing off, she took a moment to ponder the reasons behind it. Only two of her stories had made the World's front page, after months and months of trying. Ellie had indeed used every tool at her disposal to get the scoop on corruption in Alderman Sicario's office. She'd even lifted her skirt and shown a little ankle. Oh, she wasn't proud of that, but a petite figure, blonde hair, blue eyes, and long eyelashes had put some sugar on her inquisitive questions.

One man, a clerk, hadn't been able to resist Ellie's sweetness.

Frankly, she had been shocked how far she'd gotten with a few flirtatious remarks and the flash of ankle. And today, that willingness to pull out all the stops put her one up on her male counterparts.

The power was a bit intoxicating. Her star was on the rise. If a soft tone of voice, cinching her corset a bit tighter, or a playful comment opened a door only a woman could walk through, there was nothing wrong with that. Sometimes a man's gender opened doors for them. Ellie didn't see much difference.

Admitting she might be a touch full of herself but eager to tackle a new assignment, she let herself into a disappointingly spartan waiting room empty of clients. The desk where she assumed the secretary sat was also vacant. The churchlike quiet had her wondering if she'd come over too quickly.

The soft shuffle of papers from behind a door marked *PRIVATE* allayed her concern. She strode to the door, concentrating on keeping the thud of her heels quiet on the wood floor. The swishing of her skirt, however, seemed inordinately loud. Tugging on her shirtwaist, she rotated a shoulder, then knocked gently. "Hello. I'm the reporter from the World Daily News. I believe someone is expecting me."

"Yes, come in," a man said. Ellie heard a chair roll as she opened the door. A balding, middle-aged gentleman with a round face rose to greet her, shoving his watch into his pocket as he stood. "Miss Blair?"

"Yes."

They shook hands across his desk. "Glad to know ya. I'm Michael O'Toole, head of the agency." His Irish accent capped his words as thickly as the foam on a dark ale. "Fine of ye to come down and meet with me." He motioned to the corner where she was startled to see another man rising from a chair. Big, brawny, and brooding, he was rather frightening. "This is my lead detective Mr. Hanlon. Mr. Hanlon, Miss Blair."

Ellie was astonished at how small her fragile hand looked and felt in this man's paw. He did not release even a hint of a smile, but only jerked his chin slightly to acknowledge her, then returned to his chair.

"Please take a seat," Mr. O'Toole said, retaking to his.

Ellie settled on the edge again, her bustle not allowing any more of the seat. "My editor said you wanted a female reporter specifically. How can I help you, Mr. O'Toole?"

"Well, young missus, I've a predicament and I hear tell," he pointed at her for emphasis, "*you* are the duchess who can help me out." He grinned, not in a charming way, more like a snake—if a snake could grin—and leaned back in his squeaking banker's chair. "I hear you get information when others can't."

Ellie prayed her cheeks would stop their warming as she fought the rising pride. "I have scooped two other papers on a construction company with illicit ties to Alderman Sicario's office."

O'Toole's grin spread. "Aye, I heard. That was an impressive bit of sleuthing, young lady, and I want you to do more of it. For me."

Ellie cocked her head to one side. "I don't understand. Are you offering me a job as a detective?"

"Not a job. At least, not one that would require you to leave the newspaper. More like an assignment. Ye see, I currently only employ male investigators and I've a situation in which yer," his gray eyes drifted down her frame and then back up, "yer gentler qualities may be of tremendous benefit. And if you get the information I need, ye will have another scoop." He paused for the effect. "A scoop that could put the Murphy Gang away for the next century."

Ellie tightened her jaw to keep it from falling open. A scoop regarding the most powerful criminal gang on the East Coast would seal her future in journalism. A story like that would get her a job at any newspaper in the country, and for top pay. Best of all, no one would confuse Ellie Blair with that publicity hound Nellie Bly ever again. *Oh, God, thank You.*

"Are ye interested, Miss Bly?"

"I'm all ears, Mr. O'Toole. All ears."

He winked. "Good girl. Ye've the pluck and spirit of Nellie Bly, eh?"

Ellie allowed a tiny, exasperated sigh. "More, I think."

He slapped the desk. "Then I'll lay it out for ye." He reached into his middle desk drawer and withdrew a stack of letters. "A man named Sean O'Dea is said to have stolen quite a large sum of money from the Shamrock mob. We've been asked by the federal government to assist in locating the man before the Irish lads do. The government would like him to testify and if the gang finds him first—well, there won't be anything left of Mr. O'Dea." He paused slightly here, drumming his fingers on the letters. "We think we tracked him to a ranch he worked on back in the summer of '82, before he came East. Now the thing is, we don't want to spook him until we can locate the loot. Which is where ye come in."

He slid the letters over to her. Getting a go-ahead nod, Ellie picked up the stack and flipped through them. All from someone named Clegg Hoyt to a Millie Swank here in Boston.

"We intercepted some mail on its way from the ranch, trying to see, ye know, if O'Dea was reaching out to anybody or vice versa. We found Millie Swank there." He grinned like a bear eying the honey pot. "Aye, a real stroke of luck, that. She's been corresponding with the Hoyt fella. Apparently he's in the market for a mail-order bride to help him settle into his new job . . . at the *same* ranch where we believe Sean O'Dea has landed."

"My, that *was* fortunate."

"I'd like to say it was me masterful investigating skills, but sometimes—" he shrugged humbly, "well, they don't call it the luck o' the Irish for nothing. Anyhow, we've convinced Miss Swank to allow ye to pretend to be her and go to this ranch. Snoop. Find O'Dea and the money, or at least confirm that he's there."

Ellie shifted, wishing she could lean back in the chair. This was quite a lot of information to take in. "The idea is brilliant," she said more to herself than Mr. O'Toole. "No one would suspect a mail-order bride."

"Shore, that's exactly what we thought."

"I assume Mr. Hoyt and Miss Swank have never met and I match her description? At least somewhat?"

"Ye are close enough. We will pay all your expenses, and yer editor has agreed to loan ye to the agency."

She glanced again at the stack of mail. "These are the letters he wrote. How do I know what she wrote to him? I wouldn't want to get tripped up on something simple."

Mr. O'Toole nodded in admiration. "Ye are a sharp-witted girl. I see now why the newspaper racket suits ye. Ye're a fast-thinker. Well, worry not. Ye'll have a dossier to travel with. It will contain as much information as the young lady can recall sharing, as well as what we know about Sean O'Dea and this Clegg Hoyt, which is, honestly, very little, outside those letters."

"And the story is mine exclusively?"

"Sell it to every bleedin' newspaper in the country if it suits ye. We want O'Dea and the money. Period."

Ellie chewed on her bottom lip, wondering what Nellie Bly would do. Well, she knew what Nellie would do, of course. "I have just one question then."

Mr. O'Toole raised his brow, waiting.

"Where am I going exactly?"

The corner of his mouth tilted slightly. "A ranch just outside Evergreen, Wyoming."

CHAPTER 2

Ellie had thought she would not be nervous, until the train's whistle announced their approach to Evergreen. Then she felt like ants were running over her skin. She'd had days to prepare for this meeting, to plan what she would say to Mr. Hoyt, to choose her words ahead of time. Now, nothing she'd thought of seemed right. She opened the folder on her lap and again read the letter, one of several. This one, however, was her favorite.

"Dear Miss Swank, I long to ride with you across the golden prairie, down into the green valleys, and to the tops of the ancient buttes. To stand beside you as the oranges and reds of a summer sunset turn the mountain peaks to flames. To stop and let you listen to the pristine silence. To walk arm-in-arm with you, gazing up at the shimmering tapestry of the night sky. After so many letters, I feel I know you heart and soul.

"I am on my way to my new position as foreman at the Whiskey Creek Ranch. The owner says it is a pleasant place. Though the work will be hard, hours long, and the weather fickle, she advised me the ranch sits in a beautiful valley full of clear, cold streams and thick, waist-high grass. I will scout a suitable parcel out for my cabin within the first few days. I hope to find a spot with a view of the mountains, or a creek nearby. I plan to have it built by mid-August or so. You must come to Wyoming after that, if you are still so inclined. As for me, I know that if you love the wild, rugged beauty of the West as much as I do, then my search for a bride has not been in vain. Please answer as to if and when you will be arriving. I anxiously await your response. With affection, Clegg."

Ellie let out a long, slow breath. Mr. Hoyt sounded like the most decent sort of man and the way she was going to toy with him had seemed harmless back in Boston. After all, there was a greater good at stake. But now, here, perhaps only moments away from meeting him, she feared she had taken this assignment too lightly.

A criminal was on the loose, however, and this arguably was the best way to find him. His capture could well put an end to a violent, murderous criminal gang. Lives could be saved. She had to consider the greater good.

Lord, I don't want to hurt Mr. Hoyt. Please help me handle this assignment quickly and cleanly and be back in Boston as soon as possible so that he can build a life with the real Millie Swank.

The train whistled again and started slowing down for its entry into the station.

. . . and I can get back to mine. Amen.

Jim West absently noted the distant whistle announcing the train, but kept his mind on the telegram. Tapping the pencil lead on the paper, he read his words again. NEW HAND DAVE REYNOLDS FROM BAR Z BAR. TX. NEED BACKGROUND INFORMATION.

That would do it. He slid the note across the counter to ol' Moseby, the telegraph operator. Tall, skinny, gaunt as a corpse, rumor had it he'd been running this office for thirty years and was known for his uncompromising discretion. While Evergreen was not a hotbed of crime, business deals and mistresses' names were safely hidden with Moseby.

Jim fished the coins from his pocket and laid them on the counter. "You'll send that today?"

"Before two," the man said, sliding the money into the palm of his hand. "Want me to hold the reply or dispatch it?"

"Send it out to the ranch soon as you hear."

"Yes, sir."

Tipping his hat, Jim slipped out of the Western Union office and meandered down a busy boardwalk, lost in thought. Nearly a week of nosing around the ranch hadn't turned up anything, then this Dave Reynolds had applied for a job. Jim had hired him specifically because of some inconsistencies in the man's appearance and work history. After another few days, the inconsistencies had only gotten more pronounced.

Mentally, Jim ticked off the list of things that bothered him about the new hire. Reynolds had said he had just come up from working on a ranch in Texas. Yet, the man's horse wasn't trail-weary. The animal looked as if he'd ridden the train. His saddle and gear weren't new, but neither had they been used daily for six months to chase longhorns through tough Texas mesquite. Reynolds didn't have the face of a cowboy either. Only slight weathering around his eyes betrayed a vocation that did *not* take him outdoors every day. So—

Absorbed in his questions, Jim did not see the pretty little blonde standing on the boardwalk, stuffing a folder into a valise.

"Oh," she squealed as he bumped into her petite frame. Her hat flopped into her face as her feminine curves pressed against his chest. He quickly clutched at dainty shoulders to keep her from falling, but the folder slipped from her hand and papers scattered in a whirlwind to the muddy walk.

"Oh, pardon me, ma'am—"

"Oh, no," she cried, righting her hat and shoving Jim off her like he was a wet dog. She started scampering around after the documents like a panicked rabbit.

"Ma'am, my apologies." Jim crouched down to help, the papers drifting and scattering away from him as if out of meanness.

"No, no, I've got this," she said curtly. She swiped papers up in a frenzy, she and her skirt spinning like a pinwheel. The hat went sideways again, its single feather flopping madly, and a rush of golden blonde hair spilled down her back. "How did you not see me? I was standing in the middle of the boardwalk."

"Exactly. Most people are *walking* while they're on the boardwalk."

The woman shoved the papers gruffly back into the folder, making a mess of them. Some askew, most wrinkled, a few muddy. Caring only that she stopped them from blowing away.

Jim was a little insulted by her uppity tone but when a letter fluttered past his foot, he obligingly stopped it with the toe of his boot.

He reached down for the letter but she snatched it out of his hand before he could stand upright. Their eyes locked and for an instant he saw colors of blue and green that reminded him of the San Francisco bay on a sunny afternoon.

She blinked and backed away. "You're saying it's my fault you ran into me?"

"What? No." What had he said exactly? "I was a little distracted and didn't expect to walk into a pole—"

"A pole?" Her voice shot up.

"That's not what I meant either." He patted the air, trying to get Little Miss Huffy to calm down.

She shoved the folder back into her valise. "Perhaps you could just tell me where the Western Union office is?"

Pretty, but snippy. Jim shrugged mentally. No more gals like this for him. San Francisco society had ruined him on emotional, fragile women. Besides, he shouldn't be looking anyway. Not like he was staying in Wyoming long. At least he hoped not. "You're almost at it." He pointed with his thumb. "Other side of the bank."

"Thank you."

Jim tipped his hat. "Ma'am. Maybe we'll run into each other," he grinned, "I mean—see each other—again." Though he hoped not.

Her step faltered as she turned away. She didn't scowl at the joke, but Jim thought she came close. Instead, she sniffed in disapproval. With that, she was gone, pert nose in the air, the bustle on her blue dress swaying briskly, but invitingly. Too easily, he imagined running his hands through all that luxurious, golden hair—

Jim reached up and rubbed his neck. He needed to get off the ranch more. He'd spent too many sixteen-hour days with rowdy, dirty cowhands.

But that was part of the job sometimes. Living conditions he wouldn't choose for himself, companions he had to make the best of. Resigned to the situation, he gave the young lady

SNEAK PEEK

one last glance. Yeah, she was a whole lot more pleasant to look at than the boys at the Whiskey Creek Ranch.

Chuckling, but not really finding anything here funny, he decided to get lunch before heading back. Maybe a beer to go with it.

Ellie could feel the man's gaze on her but she certainly wasn't going to look back, no matter how handsome he was. She couldn't deny the strange flutter in her chest when she'd looked into his warm, brown eyes. In an instant she'd registered the dark, rugged stubble on his chin, and the unruly sprigs of brown hair poking out from beneath his hat. It curled adorably over his ears. And then he stood and he was so tall, angular, and lithe. He reminded her of a cat, a panther. He'd even moved with an uncommon grace, smooth and fluid—

Oh, for Pete's sake, she was not here for that sort of thing. *Nellie Bly doesn't get distracted by handsome cowboys. Neither will Ellie Blair. Focus.* Somewhere in the area was a man pining for his mail-order bride. Wasn't he going to be surprised when Ellie showed up?

Frowning at the joke that wasn't funny anymore, she pushed open the door to the telegraph office. She sent the message that she had arrived safely to both her editor and Mr. O'Toole, then, armed with directions from a passer-by, made her way to the hotel. Evergreen was a quaint, clean town that exuded a feeling of peace and calm. Along the busy boardwalk, she passed cowboys covered in trail dust, and residents dressed in fine shop clothes, though a year behind in style. Two soldiers eyed her appreciatively and tipped their kepis as they passed her.

The town was quite different from Boston. An odd observation, Ellie supposed, but she hadn't ever been to such a small municipality. She liked the pace—busy but not chaotic—the fact that she could see from one end of Main Street to the other, and that the sidewalks, while muddy, weren't littered with trash or spit.

Small, friendly, but she was taken aback by the noise. Yelling, whistling cowboys and the din of unhappy cattle emanated from the stockyard on the edge of town. The smell of animal waste was stronger here, but not unpleasant. Ellie preferred the way Evergreen smelled. On a hot, humid day, Boston reeked with the cloying stink of human excrement and garbage. At least this cow town in the middle of the rolling, green plains smelled more like grass and leather than urine.

Ellie signed for the hotel room and passed the fountain pen back to the clerk, a young boy wearing a visor, and garters on his sleeves. As he spun away to pluck her key from the pigeonhole, an idea struck her. People who worked in hotels often had the latest news, gossip, and details of goings-on of a community. Perhaps this young boy was no different.

"Excuse me, but I'm also looking for someone."

He rounded on her and passed her the key. "Yes, ma'am."

"I understand Mr. Clegg Hoyt works at the Whiskey Creek Ranch. You wouldn't happen to know him? Or how I could get out to the ranch?"

The boy grinned. "Aren't you in luck?"

It wasn't a question, but Ellie didn't understand the statement. "I don't know. Am I?"

"He's sittin' in our restaurant. Right there." He pointed past a towering fern to the restaurant's open double doors. A man with his back to the entrance sat alone at a table apparently eating his lunch.

Butterflies exploded in Ellie's chest. A nervous excitement thrummed in her veins. The moment was at hand . . . and she saw no reason to drag it out. *Nellie Bly wouldn't*, a voice mocked. Ellie swallowed her fear and spoke without turning back to the clerk. "Thank you." She dropped the room key in the reticule hanging from her wrist and trekked uncertainly across the lobby. Her legs had grown cold. Her heart beat wildly against her ribs. The speech she had planned danced disjointedly in her head.

She approached the man and took a deep breath. "Mr. Hoyt?" He turned slightly, looked up, and Ellie's stomach dropped. The same brown eyes. The same slightly disheveled brown hair. The same unexpected flutter in her breast.

At first he smiled, but it faltered with recognition. "It's you."

"It's me."

"From the boardwalk?"

"Yes."

An awkwardness embedded itself between them like a brick wall. He frowned, laid down his napkin with a sigh, and rose to tower over her. "Yes, ma'am. And I am Clegg Hoyt." He offered his hand.

Ellie recognized the peace offering. A fresh start. "And I . . ." *Oh, Lord, here we go.* "I am Millie Swank."

"Miss Swank." He didn't react to the name.

In her puzzlement at his dull reaction, she barely returned the shake.

"What can I do for you, ma'am?"

"I am Millie Swank." Growing insecure, she laced her hands over her stomach, waiting. Surely, he knew—

Suddenly, his square, handsome face transformed—no, melted—into an expression of horror. His eyes flew open. His mouth went slack. "Miss *Millie Swank?*" he asked carefully. "From Boston?"

"The one you have been corresponding with for a few

months now regarding the potential of matrimony. *That* Millie Swank."

Mr. Hoyt jolted, as if his knees had nearly buckled. He swallowed and motioned to the empty chair at his table. "Please, have a seat."

Puzzled, concerned her assignment might be falling apart somehow, Ellie slid into the chair. He sank down slowly opposite her, staring as if she had two heads. "I wasn't expecting you."

"I can see that." His stunned gaze roamed over her. Was he wondering if she was real? "The opportunity to visit Evergreen presented itself. I didn't have time to inform you of my plans."

"I don't know what to do with you."

"Pardon?" He'd muttered it like he meant something else.

"I mean," he shook his head, searching for words. "I'm not prepared for a wife—"

"Mr. Hoyt, I realize *you* were willing to take a bride sight unseen, but . . ."

"You weren't willing to take me the same way?"

"It sounds rather unfriendly when you say it like that. I merely thought to see if we might," Ellie shrugged a shoulder, "hit it off."

He took a deep breath and swiped a hand over his chin. For some reason, Ellie thought there was more simmering here than just matrimonial plans gone awry. *What*, she couldn't even begin to guess. But something said the man was figuring over more than just her.

He sat back, dragging his hands across the white tablecloth. "What did you have in mind, Miss Swank? Courting?"

Ellie's mouth dropped, but she closed it quickly. "No." Her turn to hem and haw, but wasn't that, after all, the way she had planned to buy time to search? By getting Mr. Hoyt to let her roam the ranch. She licked her lips. "I just thought," she spoke haltingly, carefully, "we could see if the arrangement will suit us. I'm not sure *courting* would be the right word."

He scratched his jaw. "I guess if I was expecting love I wouldn't have written to a mail-order bride."

Ellie hadn't looked at it that way. Not much of a romantic herself, she had assumed the man wanted a bride he could *come* to love. Perhaps Mr. Hoyt, in actuality, only wanted a maid and a cook, and a ranch hand—despite his decision to the close the letter *with affection*. Regardless, she had an assignment. "At the least, I should think you would want to see if we are agreeable together."

"Agreeable?" He studied her for a moment with an inscrutable expression. She could almost imagine a smile tried tweaking his lips, but she wouldn't have put money on it. "Well, I doubt Miss Stella would mind the company. She was telling me just the other day how she was anxious for my bride to show up so she could have afternoon teas and talk about needlepoint."

Ellie pursed her lips to keep from reflecting her horror at the idea. She hated few things more than frilly, silly, lady talk. "I have taken a room at the hotel. There's no need to inconvenience anyone."

"The last thing you would be is an inconvenience. Miss Stella is my employer. She lives in a large house with several guest rooms. You won't be any trouble. She's already made the offer, in fact."

Since this was better than Ellie had hoped, she dared not discourage the idea. "Well, if you're sure. I'm anxious to see the ranch about which you've written so eloquently."

His brow dove in what looked like confusion, but he quickly nodded. "Yes, the letters. I wrote you."

He didn't sound so sure. "Yes. Nearly twenty times."

He ran his tongue over his teeth and leaned forward. "You

wouldn't mind letting me read those again? Just so I can remember what all I told you. If you brought them."

"Yes, I have them. I don't think I missed any as they were blowing down Main Street."

He stared at her, but finally let a smile emerge. Charming, almost roguish, as if something was tremendously entertaining. "I guess we were destined to meet, Miss Swank. In one ... situation or the other."

Ellie's instincts told her Mr. Hoyt wasn't saying exactly what he meant. He found something funny all right, but she worried the joke might be on her.

If you'd like to find out what Jim and Ellie are up to, please pick up your copy of *Mail-Order Deception* today!

ALSO BY HEATHER BLANTON

"Heather Blanton is blessed with a natural storytelling ability, an 'old soul' wisdom, and wide expansive heart. Her characters are vividly drawn, and in the western settings where life can be hard, over quickly, and seemingly without meaning, she reveals Larger Hands holding everyone and everything together."

MARK RICHARD, EXECUTIVE PRODUCER, AMC'S HELL ON WHEELS, and PEN/ERNEST HEMINGWAY AWARD WINNER

I *love* to hear from readers. You can **find me** several different ways:

Receive a FREE book if you subscribe to my newsletter by visiting www.authorheatherblanton.com

Find me on Facebook

You can also follow me on

Bookbub

I'd also like to cordially invite you to join Heather Blanton's Readers Group on Facebook! You're welcome any time!

I love **Skyping** with book clubs and homeschool and church groups. You can always **email me** directly at heatherblanton@ladiesindefiance.com to set up a time! Thanks for reading! Blessings!

A Lady in Defiance (Romance in the Rockies Book 1)

Charles McIntyre owns everything and everyone in the lawless, godless mining town of Defiance. When three good, Christian sisters show up, stranded and alone, he decides to let them stay—as long as they serve his purposes...but they may prove more trouble than they're worth.

Hearts in Defiance (Romance in the Rockies Book 2)

Notorious gambler and brothel-owner Charles McIntyre finally fell in love. Now he wants to be a better man, he wants to know Christ. But all the devils in Defiance are trying to drag him back to the man he was.

A Promise in Defiance (Romance in the Rockies Book 3)

When scandalous madam Delilah Goodnight flings open the doors to the newest, most decadent saloon in Defiance, two good men will be forced to face their personal demons.

Daughter of Defiance (Thanksgiving Books & Blessings Book 6)

When you hit rock bottom, you have a choice: seek the light or live in the darkness. Victoria chose the darkness. Can someone like her find redemption?

Hang Your Heart on Christmas (Brides of Evergreen Book 1)

A marshal tormented by a thirst for vengeance. A school teacher desperate to trade fear for courage. They have nothing in common except a quiet, little town built on betrayal.

Ask Me to Marry You (Brides of Evergreen Book 2)

Here comes the bride...and he isn't happy. With her father's passing, Audra Drysdale accepts she needs a man to save her ranch. A mail-order groom will keep her prideful men working and a neighboring rancher at bay. What could go wrong?

Mail-Order Deception (Brides of Evergreen Book 3)

Intrepid reporter Ellie Blair gets an undercover assignment as a mail-order bride and heads off to Wyoming where she discovers her potential groom isn't what he appears to be, either.

To Love and to Honor (Brides of Evergreen Book 4)

Wounded cavalry soldier Joel Chapman is struggling to find his place in the world of able-bodied men. A beautiful but unwed woman may be his chance to restore his soul.

For the Love of Liberty

Novelist Liberty Ridley experiences an ancestor's memory from the Autumn of 1777. Stunned by the detail of it, she is even more amazed to find she's intensely drawn to Martin Hemsworth--a man dead for two centuries.

In Time for Christmas

Is she beyond the reach of a violent husband who hasn't even been born yet? Abandoned by her abusive husband on a dilapidated farm, Charlene wakes up a hundred years in the past. Can love keep her there?

Love, Lies, & Typewriters

A soldier with a purple heart. A reporter with a broken heart. Which one is her Mr. Right? A Christmas wedding could force the choice...

Hell-Bent on Blessings

Left bankrupt and homeless by a worthless husband, Harriet Pullen isn't about to lay down and die.

Grace be a Lady

Banished and separated from her son, city-girl Grace has to survive in a cowboy's world. Maybe it's time to stop thinking like a lady... and act like a man.

Locket Full of Love (Lockets & Lace Book 5)

A mysterious key hidden in a locket leads Juliet Watts and a handsome military intelligence officer on a journey of riddles, revelations, and romance.

A Good Man Comes Around (Sweethearts of Jubilee Springs Book 8)

Since love has let her down, widow Abigail Holt decides to become a mail-order bride, but with a clear set of qualifications to use in choosing her new husband. Oliver Martin certainly doesn't measure up...not by a long shot.

Made in the USA
Columbia, SC
02 November 2024